"No, I'm sure of it." Erastus drew his gaze from Kara, who was shooting Brad a killer look.

"I want a happy couple. You wouldn't believe it, but half the people who've come to buy the place were fighting and carrying on something fierce. I'd hate to think how they'd act when no one's around. A home's got to have love. Just like people."

Brad and Kara exchanged a startled glance.

"How will you know when you've met the right couple?" Brad asked, jumping in before Kara could speak.

"I just get a feeling, young man. People either look right to me or they don't, and you two look right—the perfect couple."

Kara stared at the man next to her and then back at Erastus. "We do? But you don't under—"

"Come on, honey," Brad interrupted. "Let's discuss it over here."

Honey? Kara Lawrence hardly digested the word when the drop-dead handsome stranger next to Erastus stepped forward, grabbed her elbow and yanked her away before she could utter another word.

Dear Reader,

American Romance cordially invites you to a wedding. A wedding of *convenience!*

By popular demand we're continuing our IN NAME ONLY program of marriage-of-convenience stories. In *The Newlywed Game*, Brad and Kara seemed like the "perfect couple." Only there was one small problem....

Popular historical author Bonnie K. Winn joins the Harlequin American Romance family, and we're sure you'll love her first contemporary novel.

Don't miss all the IN NAME ONLY books coming to you in the months ahead. Find out why some couples marry first...and learn to love later!

Regards,

Debra Matteucci
Senior Editor & Editorial Coordinator
Harlequin Books
300 East 42nd Street
New York, NY 10017

THE NEWLYWED GAME

Bonnie K. Winn

Harlequin Books

TORONTO • NEW YORK • LONDON
AMSTERDAM • PARIS • SYDNEY • HAMBURG
STOCKHOLM • ATHENS • TOKYO • MILAN
MADRID • WARSAW • BUDAPEST • AUCKLAND

Dedicated to Jane Jordan Browne—an agent without equal.
You made it possible.

Acknowledgments
To Harry Gray Browne, M.D., of Rancho Las Plumas de los
Avestruces for your invaluable assistance and expert
knowledge of the ostrich industry.
And to Bonnie Crisalli. Thank you for working with me to
direct and shape this book. I appreciate the "magic."

ISBN 0-373-16624-9

THE NEWLYWED GAME

Copyright © 1996 by Bonnie K. Winn.

Chapter One

They looked like the perfect couple. Almost like the figurines on the top of a wedding cake. Erastus Jones sized them up. Yep, these might be the ones to buy his ranch, the Rocking J. His and Sarah's home for the past fifty years. He had turned down a dozen offers already. The money wasn't important.

But the people were. Among all the people attending the open house, the couple approaching him looked just right, even if they didn't know it yet. He grinned to himself, thinking of Sarah smiling and nodding in agreement. Erastus straightened up, wondering if the tide had finally turned. It was wearing on him, not being able to settle the ostrich ranch in the right hands.

He gazed at the couple, both looking earnest and equally determined. Erastus swallowed a chuckle. *This should be fun.* They were well matched, the man tall and dark, the woman also tall, a leggy blond beauty who was a striking foil for the handsome man at her side. Erastus let the smile that simmered inside escape as he spoke. "Howdy. I'm Erastus Jones. I saw you from across the room. You folks interested in the ranch?"

The man and woman looked at each other and back at Erastus. They answered simultaneously. "Yes." Then each turned, staring at the other with surprise that was rapidly developing into antagonism.

Erastus purposely ignored their reactions. "Good."

The woman leaned forward earnestly, capturing his attention. "The Rocking J is perfect. I've looked at every ranch within driving distance of the city and nothing compares. As soon as I saw it, I fell in love. It was as though I'd finally come home." She glanced around with affection. "I already feel as though it's mine."

"I feel the same way," the man beside her countered, leveling her a glare.

The woman ignored him. "The ranch fits in exactly with my plans."

The man turned back to Erastus. "Mine, too. And I won't be making a lot of changes. I like the ranch just the way it is."

Incensed, the woman flashed her incredible green eyes. "I didn't say anything about making any changes."

The man shared a conspiratorial smile with Erastus. "I haven't met a woman yet who didn't change everything she touched."

"My Sarah was that way," Erastus agreed with a wizened chuckle, one hand brushing over the riot of thick white hair barely contained beneath a healthy-size western hat. His chin, covered by an explosion of cotton-colored whiskers, wriggled in accompanying amusement. "But the world was better for her changes."

The woman smiled a tad victoriously. She and the man were like two wary predators after the same prey.

And now they were clearly getting territorial about that prey. Sizing them up, Erastus contained his glee. Sarah would definitely approve of his intentions. He was sure of it.

"I'm prepared to make a firm offer for the property," the man said as he pulled his briefcase forward.

"I was going to say the same thing." The woman's voice rose as her gaze swung angrily toward the man.

"Glad to hear it," Erastus announced. "I want the place to go to a couple who'll love it like me and my Sarah did." His bright blue gaze darted between them, missing little. "Single people tend to drift. When I sell the ranch, I want to make sure it's going to someone who'll put down roots."

The man stuck out his hand. He was a tall, good-looking sort, but he also had a look about him, one that Erastus recognized with a bit of shock. It was the same look Erastus had worn himself when he'd first laid eyes on the Rocking J. A possessiveness, not one of greed, but of something that ran deeper. "I'm Brad Holbrook, sir."

Erastus accepted the firm handshake. "Good to meet you." He turned to the woman at Brad's side, his curiosity about her piqued. "You, too, ma'am."

"Kara—"

"So, you think you want to sell to a couple?" Brad interrupted.

"No, son. I'm sure of it." Erastus drew his gaze from Kara, who was shooting Brad a killer look. This couple had definite potential. "Yep. Fact is, I'd about given up on finding someone who was right for the place." He watched them both carefully, knowing his words were at odds with their behavior and believing in the twosome despite the disparity. "I want a happy couple. You wouldn't believe it, but half the people who've come to buy the place were fighting and carrying on something fierce. I'd hate to think how they act when no one's around. A home's got to have love. Just like people."

Brad and Kara exchanged a startled glance.

"Is this a condition of the sale?" Brad asked, disbelief coating his words.

"Yep. Matter of fact, I'm willing to give the right couple a good price. No haggling." Erastus watched as Kara shuffled her feet, disappointment chasing over her delicate features.

"How will you know when you've met the right couple?" Brad asked, jumping in before Kara could speak. However, her body language made it clear that she wasn't going to keep quiet for long.

"Hard to say, young man. I just get a feeling. Kind of like I'm having now."

"Now?" Kara echoed.

"Yes, ma'am. People either look right to me, or they don't and you two look right—the perfect couple."

Kara stared at the man next to her and then back at Erastus. "We do?"

Erastus's gaze narrowed. "Yep. I'd like to sell the place to you two. How's the price sound?"

Kara hesitated. "It's more than I intended to pay, but—"

"Price isn't all that important to me. If you like the place, it's yours for fifty thousand under the posted price."

"But—" Kara began.

"All right," Erastus conceded. "Seventy-five thousand under. Like I said, selling the ranch to the right couple is what's important to me."

"But you don't under—" Kara started to say again.

"Come on, honey," Brad interrupted. "Let's discuss it over here."

Honey? Kara Lawrence hardly digested the word when the drop-dead handsome stranger next to Erastus stepped forward, grabbed her elbow and yanked her away before she could utter another word.

"What are you doing?" she muttered as Brad hauled her over to the far corner of the room.

"Did you hear what he just offered?" Brad asked, not releasing her arm.

Refusing to acknowledge the effect of his touch, the lingering sensation still chasing through her body, she answered, hoping her voice was calm. "Yes. He wants a married couple to buy the ranch, which leaves me out." Kara knew she would do almost anything to get the ostrich ranch of her dreams, but ... marriage!

"What an opportunity!" Brad released her arm and raked one hand through tousled, dark hair, a thread of longing lacing his next words. "You don't know how much I want this ranch."

Kara wondered why he had dragged her away to impart this news. She wouldn't be able to purchase the Rocking J, perfect as it was. It was hard to believe that in such a short time she'd come to think of the ranch as her own. Now those dreams had been shot down by the whims of an eccentric old man. "If you're married, it looks like you stand a good chance of getting the place, then."

Brad grimaced. "But I'm not."

Her eyebrows lifted in feigned uninterest, even as she studied the slash of his dark brows, the roughly hewn angles of his far too handsome face, the piercing ebony eyes. "Then I guess you're out of the running, as well."

"Maybe not."

And maybe he was a nut case. Erastus Jones had been very specific and also totally unmovable. He was selling the most ideal ostrich ranch near Houston only to a stable, married couple. One he liked. It was too bad he had mistaken them for a married couple, but she could straighten out the mistake. And at the same time perhaps she could approach Erastus about the merits of selling the ranch to an individual. One who could equally appreciate the value of hearth and home. Her territorial instincts had been engaged and they weren't fading. She wasn't going to give up on the battle that easily. Not until she was sure Mr. Jones couldn't be persuaded to change his mind.

"Good luck on getting married in the next ten minutes," she offered caustically.

"So, am I in luck?"

A pity, she thought, that someone so incredibly good looking was obviously certifiably crazy. She backed away. "You'll have to excuse me now."

He grabbed her hands again, effectively blocking her escape. He'd spent two-thirds of his life waiting to fulfill this dream and he wasn't going to let a little thing like the lack of a wife stop him now. "I know how crazy this sounds, and no, I haven't escaped from the nearest asylum. But, I want this place and, from what I heard you tell Mr. Jones, you do, too. What I'm proposing is a partnership."

Her eyebrows narrowed suspiciously. "Why should I want to go into a partnership with you?"

"Are you looking for a place close to Houston?"

"Well, yes, but—"

His eyes swept over her, obviously assessing her monetary worth. "And haven't most of them been way out of sight? Unless they're several hundred miles farther out of the city?"

Cautiously she nodded her head, not forgetting that this man wanted *her* ostrich ranch.

"And this one already has incubators, brooders, pens." Brad ticked the items off one at a time on tapered, well-formed fingers, but his eyes reflected far more, as though he were thinking of something other than the practical items he listed. "The place is large enough, it's close to the city, and the land is perfect. Not to mention the fact that Mr. Jones is willing to slice seventy-five thousand off the price."

"And maybe it's the same deal he'd give to the *right* single person," Kara answered as she spun around to view the house once again.

"What's that supposed to mean?" Brad asked with a suddenly narrowing gaze.

"Perhaps he was just trying to get rid of you," Kara retorted as she pivoted back to face the wariness in his expression. "After all, I saw this place first."

"First?" Unmistakable anger crept over his face. "Considering I've been looking the place over for the past twenty years, I don't think so." And considering that he already felt the place was his once he'd decided to buy it, Brad resented her thinking that she could somehow twist Mr. Jones around her pretty little finger.

"Twenty years?" she repeated in disbelief.

A different expression, one that briefly resembled longing before it fled, took over his face. "Since I was twelve years old, yes. And I'm not giving up *my* ranch to the first upstart that comes along."

"Upstart?" Inflamed, she didn't notice her voice rising. "I'll have you know that I've been canvassing property for months. My savings are dwindling faster than interest rates are rising. I walked away from my job and collected my pension fund to pay for this place. Since then I've looked at every overpriced ranch within sight of Houston, and believe me this is the *only* ranch worth considering. I may not have been mooning over the Rocking J for twenty years, but I didn't suddenly have a whim to go into the ostrich business, either!" Not to mention the proprietary air she'd felt in stepping off every foot of the ranch, envisioning it as her own home. She didn't plan to let this infuriating man simply snatch it away.

"Walking out on your job was a well-thought-out idea?" Brad's voice was dry, the mocking tone clearly indicating his opinion of such an act.

Despite her penchant for impulsiveness, it had been an uncharacteristic move, one she sometimes regretted, except when she thought of returning to her nine-to-five grind. "That's hardly any of your business. The fact is I've researched this property thoroughly." She pulled out a prospectus on the Rocking J from the depths of her purse. "Unlike you, I didn't rush in off the street because I saw a For Sale sign."

"If I'd known the old guy was willing to sell, I'd have been here sooner," he retorted with undisguised exasperation.

Kara smiled sweetly. "But you didn't." Her grin deepened, purposely baiting him. "So I saw it first!"

Brad's gaze deliberately raked over her totally inappropriate silk dress that wisped around impossibly long legs and dipped at the neckline like an invitation to disaster. He would enjoy accepting that invitation, he admitted silently, but they were firmly rooted in warring camps. His gaze continued to roam as he stared at the ankle-breaking high heels she wore that were barely more than scant, provocative bits of leather emphasizing her remarkable legs. Hardly ranch gear.

He watched her nervously flip her long strawberry blond hair over one shoulder. She completed the motion as he spoke in a mocking tone, his gaze still roving over her. "I suppose you think *you* can run a ranch?"

She followed his dismissive gaze and then flushed. "I dressed to *buy* a ranch, not run one!" Defensively she gripped her purse tighter. "Questioning my qualifications doesn't change the fact that this is *my* ranch!" she hissed.

"You two still talking over the price, I see." Erastus clapped a hand on Brad's shoulder and met their startled expressions, barely concealing the twinkle in his own eyes. "I don't want to rush you, but a crowd of bidders is gathering."

Kara and Brad stared at each other in hostile dismay.

Erastus didn't seem to notice. "You remind me a lot of me and my Sarah." His eyes took on a faraway gaze. "Always full of spirit, Sarah was. Sassy, spunky." He laughed, obviously caught up in his memories. "She wouldn't have given in just 'cause I wanted something, either. But, maybe you can talk your lady into the place, son." Ignoring Kara's gasp,

Erastus winked conspiratorially at Brad. "The fiery spirit keeps 'em lively."

Kara managed a weak smile, unwilling to antagonize Mr. Jones and equally unwilling to forgo her last chance. "Are you certain you'll only sell to a couple? After all, there are single people who would make this their home and treasure the ranch as much—"

"I'm sure there are, little lady, but that's not what I want for the Rocking J. It's a special place and my Sarah wouldn't rest easy knowing I hadn't taken care that it went only to the right couple."

Kara sighed while Brad spoke. "We're still talking it over."

"Like I said, I don't want to rush you. Unless, of course, you don't think it's a good deal," Erastus added, before moving on.

"Like we wouldn't think it's a good deal," Kara muttered.

"The place is a steal," Brad admitted.

Their eyes met as they grudgingly measured each other.

"You're forgetting one thing," she reminded him grimly. "We're not married."

Brad stared at his opponent as Erastus circulated through the room. "We could be for the duration of the deal."

She kept her mouth from dropping open with an effort. What a gallant proposal, especially coming from this hardheaded man. "I don't think so."

"You're saying you have plenty of time to keep looking for the right ranch?" Brad goaded her, having just heard her own admission that her time was running out.

Brad moved a bit closer, and she sucked in her breath. Up close he was even more devastatingly attractive than she had first surmised. Dangerous, her mind screamed, despite his annoying arrogance.

She flushed, then decided to play his game. "And just how did you plan to convince Mr. Jones that we're married?"

"That should be easy enough." The silky tone in his voice sent a shiver through her unsuspecting body and instantly she remembered his touch on her arm, her equally disquieting response.

Annoyed with her own reaction, Kara's gaze grew skeptical. She wanted to believe that Brad was that too-handsome breed, the kind that didn't have much in the brains department, since all his genes had obviously been occupied in creating a physically superior specimen. "Mr. Jones doesn't look that easily duped."

Brad's ebony gaze raked over her. "Did you actually tell him we weren't married?"

He wasn't dull witted, unfortunately. "Well...no."

Kara could see Brad's careful control over his emotions. His anger was still there, but apparently it was overwhelmed by his desire to own the ranch. From his own admission, a powerful twenty-year desire.

"And you were planning to place a bid if Jones hadn't put in that ridiculous stipulation?" Brad persisted.

A glance out the window at the perfect setting reinforced Kara's desire to own the place. She had spent far too long already searching for a place that suited her needs, all the while depleting her savings. Much longer and her dream would be out of reach.

Her options were dwindling daily. Facing the truth, she knew she didn't really have a choice, other than to find another job and reenter the rat race.

Even so, she didn't want to share her dream with Brad Holbrook. Unable to explain the territorial feeling that had gripped her when she'd first set foot on the ranch, she only knew she already considered the place hers. Not the interloper's who now waited expectantly for her answer.

"Yes, I planned to make a bid." She steeled her voice, leaving no doubt about her intentions. "And I still want the Rocking J—for myself."

Brad met her defiant glance and returned it firmly. "Don't get your hopes up and think that I'm going to be gallant and leave the path clear for you."

A loud noise from the other bidders captured Kara's attention, and she sighed in disappointed resignation as she angled her head toward the people bunched close to Mr. Jones. "I don't think it would matter if either of us steps aside. Look at all the people still bidding."

Brad's gaze narrowed. "But do they suit Mr. Jones's specifications like we do?"

"Us?" she asked in disbelief. "We're the furthest thing from what he wants!"

"He doesn't know that."

Kara hesitated. "It doesn't seem right. He's sincere about carrying out his late wife's wishes."

Brad snorted. "We wait any longer, he'll find another 'perfect couple' and we'll have lost out on the opportunity of a lifetime. The old guy's got to be bats. Never having seen us before and deciding we're the example of loving marrieds. Look, here come two more couples. You want him to decide they're better candidates?''

''If only we had more time to think this through, discuss our options....''

''I'll lay it on the line.'' His dark gaze captured hers and she suppressed an involuntary shiver. ''I want this ranch. You want this ranch. We can buy it together, or we both lose. You going to let your stiff-necked pride get in the way?''

Briefly she wondered if he was this intense about going after everything he wanted. ''Mine? What about you and your twenty-year hold on the ranch?''

''We can work out all the legalities with our lawyers later, right of buyout, partnership agreement. But right now we've got to convince Mr. Jones that we're a loving, married couple.''

Looking at him, Kara bit back a gulp of apprehension, even though she knew she'd never stumble on another opportunity like this one. ''But—''

''Are you willing or not?'' The noise from the bidding accelerated.

Devastating, dangerous and determined. That's what he was. Yet she didn't relinquish her lingering anger. ''If it's the only way—''

Brad didn't let her finish. Instead he grabbed her hand and they raced back to the spot where Mr. Jones stood, along with his real estate agent.

Brad raised his hand. ''We'd like to make an offer.''

''That's what I was waiting to hear.'' Erastus beamed, sounding relieved, the twinkle in his eye now visible.

The agent puckered his brow in a frown as he studied them. ''I don't believe I've met you.''

Glancing down at Kara with an adoring expression, Brad supplied the introduction. "We're Mr. and Mrs. Brad Holbrook."

She could feel the heat rising in her cheeks. How would Brad look if he really meant that loving introduction?

The wily real estate agent conducting the sale obviously knew that he had a captive, eager audience. Something about a seller's market scented the air with blood, sending sharks like this agent into a frenzy. And it was clear that the man wanted to hold out for the best offer.

But Erastus Jones ignored the real estate broker and smiled at Kara and Brad, his wizened features rearranging themselves with pleasure. "So, you want to fill the Rocking J with love."

Stumbling, Kara couldn't form an appropriate answer. But Brad smoothly stepped into the gap. "It'll be a great home, full of possibilities."

"I suppose you'll be wanting to fill the place with babies?" Erastus continued.

Kara turned to Brad, but for once he, too, seemed at a loss. She could feel the heat stain her cheeks. *Babies!*

Erastus cackled, a satisfied sound. "You'll have years to work on that, my boy. No need to be embarrassed, little lady. You'll see that, too, in time. My Sarah and me wanted lots of babies, but it wasn't to be." He shook his head at the mounting memories. "But there can still be happiness. Wasn't anyone happier than Sarah and me." The glint returned to his eyes. "But this isn't our time, it's yours."

"If our offer's accepted," Brad observed quietly, not wanting to tread on the other man's memories.

"There's no question about that. It's yours," Erastus boomed, his voice drowning out the others in the room.

The real estate agent turned in disgust and threw up his hands, stalking away from the disappointed group of bidders to retrieve his briefcase.

Kara wasn't sure why, but despite the older man's eccentric insistence on having only a married couple buy his ranch, she liked Erastus's down-home charm. That, and the fact that he must have loved his wife very much to demand that their home be passed on to an equally loving couple. It was an incredibly sweet gesture, one that tore at her heart. How must it feel to have such an encompassing love? She didn't have time to linger with the thought since Brad began talking contracts.

The real estate agent didn't seem pleased, but at a look from Mr. Jones, he produced the papers from his briefcase and laid them out on the desk, indicating where they should sign.

Kara reached for the pen when Brad clamped down on her hand. "Not yet, honey. We should have our lawyers look over the papers."

"I imagine that's a good idea these days," Erastus Jones agreed. "Never know what kind of polecat's crawling into the cave next to yours."

"I'll sign an agreement of intent," Brad offered, whipping out his own pen. "That makes our offer legal until we get everything checked over."

Kara watched in confusion, wondering what the fast-thinking Brad Holbrook was up to next. After he had signed the paper, he turned to her, offering his arm.

Dredging up a smile for Erastus, Kara walked outside with Brad, turning to him as soon as they were out of sight. "What was that for? I thought you were in such a hurry to cement the deal."

"I didn't bother to ask your last name, but I don't suppose it's Holbrook," he replied.

"Of course not. It's Lawrence. But what does..." She glanced up, meeting his ebony eyes. "Oh. The papers."

His expression remained even. "I'll admit I didn't think of it either until you reached for that pen."

"But what will we do?"

"Get married, of course."

Chapter Two

Eloping with a total stranger hadn't been jotted down in Brad's planner. But then he had never expected to find a green-eyed, golden-haired beauty to wed that day. The fact that those eyes were now flashing with undisguised fire only heightened his awareness of her. He doubted the ostriches they planned to raise would kick as much as she had.

Especially when he had told her their destination. To his consternation, Brad had discovered that Texas required a three-day waiting period to get married. But Nevada, now that was a state for people in a hurry.

His alternative, spur-of-the-moment plan had infuriated Kara so much she hadn't even noticed the plane he'd booked for them. It apparently hadn't registered with her that he owned the air charter business. Holbrook Enterprises was plastered on the hangar they drove into at Hobby Airport, but she was concentrating on letting him know what she thought of his bizarre idea, arguing the madness of his plan the entire time.

His chief pilot taxied the airplane out onto the runway as they fastened their seat belts. Brad had arranged to ride with a shipment destined for Los

Angeles. His personal airplane was down for mainte-
nance, so he'd hitched them on this cargo charter. No
problem when you owned the company.

"Las Vegas?" she questioned again, as though unable to believe she was sitting in an airplane, going
along with his plan.

"No blood test, no waiting period. We just show up,
sign some papers, say a few words—"

"And we're married." Shock seemed to be replacing fire.

"It's not like it's for real." Brad wondered for a
moment if it was disappointment he saw in her eyes,
but then dismissed the notion.

"Of course not." Kara fiddled again with the seat
belt. "I just..." Her eyelids flickered shut briefly, then
opened to meet his glance defiantly.

"Why don't you rest for a while? We'll be there in
a few hours. I'll wake you when it's time to land."

She held his gaze for a long moment before jerking
away to stare out the window. "All this for a ranch,"
she muttered.

Deciding he'd better retreat before she backed out
or started arguing again, Brad escaped across the aisle
to pull down a table and get to work. It would be early
evening when they landed. He needed time to prepare
the avalanche of agreements and partnership papers
for the following day.

The changing terrain passed beneath them and Brad
continued to ignore his reluctant bride-to-be. When
they neared the airport, he dispatched the papers to his
briefcase and returned to the seat next to hers. But
Kara hadn't slept as he had hoped. Instead she stared
out the window.

For a moment he was afraid she might have changed her mind. And he hated to admit how much this venture meant to him. It would be difficult to explain to anyone the sense of rightness he felt when on the Rocking J. Ever since the first time he'd accidentally stumbled across its boundaries, he'd felt an immediate sense of belonging. His childhood friend, whose family owned a place near the Rocking J, continued to invite Brad for visits, keeping his interest in the Rocking J alive. Brad had thought he might lose his desire for the place, but it had only intensified as he matured. Discreet inquiries had always borne the same disappointing results—the Rocking J wasn't for sale at any price.

Until now.

Brad focused on his unlikely partner. Her profile was turned toward him and he noted, not for the first time, the elegant bones of her face, the pert nose, the stubborn chin. But his eyes lingered on the soft flush of her cheeks, the beguiling shape of her lips. Which were turned downward in a frown, he noted. From his vantage point, he could also see those incredible legs and some provocative-looking curves.

She glanced up, but he didn't look away, unable to disguise the interest in his gaze. He saw her pale skin flush, then the darkening of her unusual eyes into an emerald as deep as the forests they'd left behind.

Purposely he made his voice brisk. "We'll be landing in a few minutes. I've arranged for a car."

"Then it won't be long?"

He thanked his lucky stars that she seemed propelled by shock. Even if she demanded an annulment as soon as reality sank in, they would be able to buy the ranch. From all the resistance she had put up before he had whisked her into his airplane, he had a feeling she would be a formidable opponent again soon. Seeing the resolute set to her face, he guessed that prickliness was reviving even now. He met captivating green eyes that glinted with the gold of untold wealth.

"No, it won't be long. In about an hour we'll be married."

HIS MOUTH WAS HARD, his lips gentle as they pressed against hers. The mandatory kiss wasn't perfunctory as she had expected. Instead every repressed emotion she possessed reeled as his lips molded to hers. It was all for show, she reminded herself as she was crushed against the unyielding expanse of a broad, muscled chest. Even so, she was grateful for the support of his arms as he stepped away while still holding her. Kara tried to maintain a calm expression as her eyes inadvertently caught Brad's. There was an unexpected light in his gaze, one that surprised as much as intrigued her.

Stunned, she realized this cartoon wedding was off to a booming start when a heart-shaped, red neon sign began blinking "Love Forever" as the organist tapped out notes that sounded strangely like the beginning of a "charge" march at a sports event.

In seconds, Kara guessed the purpose behind the bizarre musical selection. A flock of molting doves burst from an overhead cage that was suspended by gold-tasseled ropes. Feathers flew as the birds swooped around the room.

"I had to ask for the deluxe package," Brad muttered.

Kara hadn't thought anything could make her even smile after the stressful afternoon, but she had to bite her lip to keep from laughing out loud at the ridiculousness of the situation.

"Congratulations, Mr. and Mrs. Holbrook." The minister, who happened to be an Elvis impersonator, spoke with practiced ease as they parted.

The enthusiastic organist switched songs and burst into a chorus of yet another Elvis tune. The two hired witnesses acted as backup singers as they crooned the accompanying doo-wahs.

As Brad moved away with the Elvis-cloned minister, Kara stared at her gaudily garbed finger. A pink cubic zirconium ring hastily obtained at the counter in the chapel made her lips twitch. While not a materialistic person, she wryly acknowledged that she wasn't exactly dripping in diamonds. There had been no time for niceties like real rings.

The kiss, however, had been very real. Unconsciously she rubbed her fingers over her lips. The unexpected tingle of Brad's kiss lingered. She had expected to feel nothing. Instead, the light touch, the imprint of his full, warm lips had been more potent than the knowledge that she had actually married a stranger.

Glancing up, she watched Brad pay the proprietor of the Love Me True Wedding Chapel, their conversation a muted noise in the background. She looked around the tacky room. Plastic flowers rested in chipped, gold-spray-painted urns. A metal arch decorated with faded, drooping bows was sent into frizzy relief by fluorescent lights that blinked out the wedding chapel's message through the long, low window.

Bright red carpet covered the floor, while the walls were painted Pepto-Bismol pink.

Stifling a giggle, she decided it looked like a set from an overdone Dolly Parton movie. One with an exceptionally poor set director. Although aware that people really did run off to Vegas to get married, she had never expected to find herself standing in just such a ridiculous-looking place.

And married to a stranger.

Needing to stay close to Houston, unwilling to return to the confines of a regular job, she had jumped without thinking. Not for the first time. Perhaps she could just tear up the papers, pretend this had never happened. The script for this comedy could be rewritten, the director could call "cut," and she would be off the hook. Then she and Dolly Parton could retreat to their dressing rooms, have a good laugh. But Brad was walking toward her.

"Sorry about this place." He grimaced at the fake arbor of bows and dusty flowers. "I didn't know it was this bad. I asked for directions to the nearest chapel. I think it's stretching the point to call this a chapel. But, it got the job done."

Her voice sounded distant even to her ears. "Yes, it did."

"I'd like to suggest a wedding supper, but we need to head back to Houston, so we can get a partnership agreement drawn up and be ready to see Mr. Jones in the morning. I sketched out a preliminary arrangement, but we need to have it checked by our lawyers."

"Of course." It wasn't like a real wedding, she reminded herself. And the Hollywood prop ceremony hardly conjured the desire for a celebration, especially since she intended to have the ending rewritten.

As they turned to leave, the woman who had played the organ approached them, her face wreathed in smiles. "Good luck to you both."

Kara and Brad murmured thank-yous.

"I've been doing this for years and I've never seen such a perfect couple," she continued. "I know you won't be one of those that gets hitched in Vegas and then divorced just as quickly." She shook her head, a twinkle in her eyes. "Nope, you've got the look of them that last. Well, all the best to you!"

Kara and Brad raised startled eyes to each other. She was the second person in twelve hours to declare them a "perfect couple."

After leaving the chapel, they were headed toward the car when the woman ran after them and tossed handfuls of rice. The white grains showered them thoroughly. The old-fashioned gesture brought a sting of tears to Kara's eyes. This was for business, she reminded herself. Just because she had always dreamed of her wedding day didn't mean this one counted. But you had only one first wedding day, she thought, wishing she could undo what she'd just done.

Brad reached to brush the clinging rice from her hair. His hand lingered, the deep color of his eyes darkening even further to a sooty coal.

He cleared his throat, his voice sounding unnaturally husky. "I think that got most of them."

Her hand reached up unconsciously to check her hair. But the sensation of his touch remained. Like a heat wave, it singed a path that continued to send stirring waves. For a moment, she had an insane desire to touch the tumble of dark hair at his forehead. But her hand fell away.

"Thank you." Was that her voice? Sounding unnaturally high, nearly breathless?

His tone turned brisk, almost purposely so, as he checked his watch after opening the car door. "We're due at the airport now."

She climbed inside the car and he shut the door. Nice manners, she thought. At least she hadn't married a barbarian.

Married!

The word stuck in her thoughts like a persistent cog in a broken-down machine. Reevaluating the past few hours, she decided she was the one who was certifiable. In all of her twenty-six years, she'd never done anything so impulsively crazy.

Surely there had been a solution other than marrying a total stranger. But thoughts of her mother intruded. Kara couldn't leave the Houston area where her mother lived alone. And regrettably, even if she had swallowed her pride, she couldn't return to the job she had stalked away from.

Kara had racked her brain since they'd boarded the plane, hoping for an alternative, but she had come up empty. Which left her in a rented car speeding toward the Vegas airport. Married to a handsome man—no make that an Adonis of a man—whom she knew nothing about.

The clear night cast no shadows; instead the sky was blanketed with luminescent stars and a golden full moon.

A night for lovers.

The thought intruded, unwanted, unneeded.

"We'll be at the airport soon." Brad turned the wheel and sped down the street which was busy even at the late hour. It was like the entire city, a twenty-four-hour pulsating live wire. Exhilarating, but also exhausting, and Kara was ready to leave it behind.

When they reached the airport, Brad drove confidently to a hangar on the west side. After parking, he escorted her to a plane. She noted absently that the plane was emblazoned with the same logo as the one on which they had arrived. Even with her rudimentary knowledge about aircraft, she knew it wasn't the same plane. It occurred to her that it was strange that he had chartered a plane for their trip. Commercial flights were easily available.

"Chuck, let's get moving," Brad began as soon as they boarded the airplane.

"Ready when you are."

"Good. You'll have to double back as soon as we hit Houston and load that second shipment."

Kara listened to their conversation in growing confusion.

Brad escorted her to the one row of seats behind the cockpit. "We're all set."

"You acted as though you were giving the orders up there."

He shrugged. "It's my airplane."

"Yours? But I thought it belonged to an air charter company."

"Mine, as well. Don't worry. The pilot's good." Brad's white teeth were a slash in his tanned face. "Not as good as I am, of course."

She nodded, shockingly aware of how little she knew about Brad Holbrook. "And you'll have time to run an ostrich ranch?"

Brad shrugged. "The charter business pretty much runs itself. I have a great general manager and the best pilots in the business."

She was churning this new information over when he reached for her hand. The unexpected contact stunned her. "Look, I'm sorry about all this. The crude chapel, rushing you back here without even dinner. I did ask Chuck to pick up something to eat. It's hardly wine and roses, but..." He released her hand to retrieve some white sacks. "I didn't know what you liked so there's Chinese *and* Mexican."

A silly lump stuck in her throat. "Sounds like a great combo."

"Actually, it's probably a guarantee for heartburn, but you won't starve."

"I wasn't all that hungry."

"It'll be midnight by the time we get back to Houston. You'll need your strength. Tomorrow will be a big day."

She nodded, accepting the carton of Mongolian Beef he handed her.

"And there's an even longer night stretching out in front of us."

Startled by his words and the vision they created, she dropped the carton, then scrabbled to retrieve the chunks of beef and broccoli that had escaped her shaking hands.

"Let me get that." Efficiently he retrieved her spilled dinner.

She watched his long, strong fingers as they reassembled the carton of food. Feeling like an absolute idiot, she accepted her dinner and then stared at it without a bit of interest. She stirred her fork around, rearranging the food several times as Brad ate his own meal. Surely she had misinterpreted his remark about the coming evening.

"I'm going to relieve Chuck for a while." He collected the cartons. "Finished?"

She nodded.

"Why don't you try to get some sleep?"

He rose and she watched his retreating back. Although exhausted, she doubted she would sleep a peaceful night until she ended this farce. The sooner the better.

BRAD RUBBED at dry, unseeing eyes. Too much had transpired that day to leave an ability for concentration.

Chuck Foxworth returned to his seat, slipping on his headset. In his late forties, he was a rugged man. Only a slash of silver at his temples revealed his age. With his chestnut hair and piercing blue eyes he didn't look nearly fifteen years older than Brad. Tall, commanding in his own way, he liked the independence of piloting. Especially with a boss like Brad who let him run his own show as chief pilot. "Everything's shipshape. We should be able to unload, reload and be back in the air in an hour."

"Good. Tom's waiting at the hangar."

"So how's the bridegroom holding up?"

"Very funny."

"I'm not the one who married a girl he'd never met before today."

Brad shoved a hand through tousled hair. "Tell me about it. But what an opportunity."

Chuck let out a low wolf whistle. "No kidding."

An unexpected shaft of resentment asserted itself. "Knock it off. This is strictly business."

"More's the pity."

"I'd hate to have to rearrange your bones."

"I smell trouble, boss. If this is strictly business, somebody forgot to tell you."

Brad slipped his headset off, arching a brow at Chuck. "I'm going to check on Kara."

Chuck wisely withheld comment as Brad headed back in the cabin.

Not having really expected her to take his suggestion, he was surprised to see that Kara had fallen asleep. Her head was tilted at an uncomfortable, awkward angle. But it didn't diminish her grace. Nor her beauty.

Those stunning green eyes were concealed by a sweep of dark lashes that shadowed her pale skin. He was struck by how vulnerable she looked in her sleep. Even when she had seemed to be operating in a state of shock, he had never sensed anything but strength. Only a very determined woman would agree to marriage to achieve her ambitions. He admired the ability to separate sentimentality from practicality.

But, now...she seemed almost fragile. Perhaps it was a trick of his overactive imagination. A passing fancy that gathered momentum as the dark night slid by.

Then she stirred, unfolding like the clouds scuttling through the sky. And the magnetism of her gaze caught him as she fixed incredible eyes on him. But it was her words that threw him.

"Get this, Mr. Holbrook. There's no way I'm spending the night with you."

Chapter Three

In the broad and embarrassing light of day, Kara wished she could recall the words she had tossed out at Brad the previous night. But he seemed determined to ignore them, and she would, too. Even if it dented every bit of her pride.

Erastus Jones fairly beamed at them. "I'd like to show you the whole place. I know you'll be discovering a lot on your own, wanting to fix things up, maybe even change others." He nodded sagely. "I understand that. We wanted to put our mark on the place, too. Hell, my father never would have expected me to turn this into a bird ranch. Back when he was in charge, it was strictly cattle. But times change. And you have to keep up."

Erastus laughed, a deep, rich sound. "Sarah just wanted a few birds at first, to try them out. She had such a good time with the first round of chicks, we kept adding more of them. Next thing you know, we had some financial reverses, had to sell part of the land. That was nearly forty years ago. It was a good thing by then we were raising ostriches. There wouldn't have been enough land left for the cattle."

"It's still a good-sized spread," Brad commented.

"Yep."

"It's a beautiful place," Kara murmured, listening to the swish of live oak leaves, the gentle rustle of the towering pines.

"That it is," Erastus agreed. "It's peculiar. Even though we're close to the city, I've never felt hemmed in. Always been my piece of freedom."

"That's what I'm looking for," Kara admitted, breathing in the sweet, heavy smell of magnolia blossoms.

Brad's eyes lit with surprise. "More than an investment?"

She nodded.

Erastus glanced between them. "I expect you'll find more than you bargained for in any new place."

Kara met Brad's eyes, seeing a matching expression of unreadable emotion. They had definitely gotten into more than they had bargained for.

"Let's start with the house." Erastus led them inside and toward a comfortable room that served as a den but was large enough to hold a bar and pool table. "This has always been the heart of the place. Sarah and me spent most of our time here. Good times and bad. We worked 'em out in here." He indicated the double doors of the study that was located just beyond the den. "You probably remember there's a pool off the patio." Then he walked down the hall, pointing out various rooms. He stopped suddenly at the end of the hall. "And this is the master bedroom. Pretty important place, too."

Kara met Brad's eyes and she felt the heat creeping up her neck. There seemed no escape from the reminder of her ill-spoken words. Resolutely she firmed her shoulders, deciding to ignore the incident.

"I'm sure you'll be luckier than Sarah and me. About having kids, I mean." Shaking his head, Erastus brought himself back to the present. "Now I expect you'd like to get on with signing the papers."

"Yes, sir," Brad replied, not quite taking his gaze from Kara.

She trailed behind Erastus, aware of Brad's scrutiny, determined not to acknowledge it. Soon they were all seated around the desk in the study. Brad and Kara each reached for the copy of the offer to purchase. With a glance at Mr. Jones's observant pose, Kara deferred to Brad, even though she knew she had every bit as much right to the paper. It was confining to play such an unnatural role. Itching to read the agreement, she tried to sit quietly while Brad read through the papers.

"Mr. Jones, I'm not familiar with this addendum," Brad said, raising concerned eyes to the older man.

"What is it?" Kara glanced between them and Brad pointed out the bothersome paragraph.

It didn't take her long to figure out why. The wording specified that Mr. Jones had the right to inspect the ranch, home and its inhabitants for the next six months, to insure himself of their suitability. Her gaze caught Brad's. If that was the case, they would have to portray a loving, married couple for the next several months—or lose the ranch.

"Those are my terms," Erastus announced. "And I'm not budging."

"And the price is still what we agreed on yesterday?" Brad asked.

"Of course. I don't go back on my word. And, if in six months, I see that you're still right for the place, then it's yours, with a clear title."

"They're very unusual terms," Kara said, not wanting to offend the older man, yet not willing to carry on the pretense indefinitely. She was hoping for an annulment, not a long, drawn-out extension of this charade.

"Got two other couples that came in after you left," Erastus replied, studying the tip of his alligator boots. "They were real interested in the place."

Brad shot Kara a telling glance. If they waffled, they lost out. Taking a deep breath, she nodded her head. Gratitude swept over his face as he quickly signed his name and then handed her the pen.

And she froze.

Kara Holbrook. She was no longer Kara Lawrence. In spite of the mad dash to Vegas, and the tawdry ceremony, it hadn't seemed real. But signing her new name to these documents would finalize things. The minister's words echoed in her memory. For better or for worse.

She had taken vows. To love, honor and cherish the man who gazed at her. Forcing her hand to remain steady, she signed the unfamiliar name.

To his credit, Brad didn't snatch the paper back. Instead, he stared at her long and hard as the paper lay between them. He made his voice quiet. "Are you sure, Kara?"

She thought of the financial web that was tightening about her. One that made this arrangement necessary. "Yes."

Only then did he take the paper and give it to Erastus. It crinkled as Erastus swept his alert gaze over their signatures and then affixed his own. "I know you'll want to move in as soon as possible. Let me know if you want to keep any of the furniture. I don't need half of it. Matter of fact, I plan to leave what I can."

Kara kept from groaning aloud with only a concentrated effort. She had forgotten about the physical proximity of the move. They were going to have to live together. An equally startled look on Brad's face indicated he hadn't quite thought this out, either. Of course, they hadn't expected Mr. Jones's prohibitive restriction clause.

Meeting Brad's eyes, Kara felt her stomach sink. She had just agreed to move in and behave in a loving manner with the most attractive, and therefore dangerous, man she had ever met.

BRAD PUT MORE of his belongings in place. Fortunately there was plenty of space for all their furniture. However, vacating their apartments hadn't been easy. Nothing about the last two weeks since they'd signed the papers had been easy. But this seemed like the final, irrevocable step.

Brad had kept the same place through most of his years of building the air charter company. Leaving the apartment was like parting with an old friend. And now he faced his new roommate.

Kara had cleaned the partly empty ranch house with a fury he suspected she wished to heap on him. Luckily they hadn't come to blows yet.

Upending his favorite chair, Brad carried it into the living room, settling it in the center of the room. Stepping back, he viewed it with satisfaction. Even though he'd upgraded his other furniture as his air charter business prospered, this was one piece that had always stayed. It had taken years, but it was broken in just right, a little lumpy perhaps, but the most comfortable chair in the world.

"Yuck!"

Brad whirled around to see Kara standing, hands on hips, as she stared in disapproval, her succulent lips pursed in a frown.

He took a defensive stance in front of his old leather recliner. "What?"

"That." She pointed at the chair, quivering in distaste as though he'd emptied the refuse from the ostrich pens in the middle of the living room floor.

"What's wrong with it?"

"You're not going to leave it there, are you?"

Annoyed, he patted the well-worn leather. "And why not?"

"Well, it's...it's..." Her frown deepened. "Perhaps it's better suited to the study or the den."

"It's fine right here," Brad insisted.

"It's just so...visible," she said, trying to be tactful.

"And that isn't?" he asked, pointing to the oversize portrait of a stern, unsmiling woman that had been hung prominently over the mantel.

"That's my Great-Aunt Tillie!" Kara protested.

"Have you ever watched her eyes?" Brad asked as he approached the painting. "No matter where you go, they follow you." He demonstrated, walking across the room while staring at the portrait, which obligingly stared back.

But Kara wasn't impressed. She folded her arms militantly in front of her. "So?"

"It's uncanny. Who wants some old bat following every step they make?"

"Old bat?"

"Sorry, your Aunt Tillie. Frankly, I don't care whose picture it is. I don't like the idea of being watched."

"Maybe she's just trying to oversee the decorating of the house," Kara replied meaningfully as she closed the space between them. "Making sure it's not entirely tacky." She halted suddenly, staring at the assortment of items on the side table.

Seeing her interest, Brad volunteered their origins. "From my travels in the air charter business. I've collected pieces from all over the world."

Her eyes skipped over the items, resting on the shrunken head. "That can't be real."

If she could hang a portrait of her dead Aunt Tillie, he could display a genuine shrunken head. "Afraid so. Of course, I'd be willing to store it, if you'll do the same with Tillie."

She swallowed, then shook her head. "I don't think so." Her gaze continued on until it rested on a naked, swollen figure.

"Pre-Columbian Venus," Brad mused. "Fertility goddess."

"And you think my Aunt Tillie's bad," she muttered.

Shrugging, Brad turned, knocking into a small, circular item. It fell to the floor. Picking it up, Brad studied the object before calling to Kara. "This yours?"

"Yes, it goes on the mantel."

He turned the unusual item over, examining it. "What is it?"

"A hair wreath," she explained with undue satisfaction.

"What's that?"

"Locks of Great-Aunt Tillie's hair woven into a wreath after she died."

Brad immediately dropped the wreath and heard Kara giggle.

"That's barbaric," he accused.

"I'll admit no one thought of shrinking her head," Kara acknowledged. "But in her time, they made do with just the hair."

"You got any more little surprises like this?" Brad asked, wiping his hands against his jeans as if trying to remove any residue remaining from the hair wreath.

Kara glanced meaningfully at his collection of unusual objects. "You tell me."

Instead he angled his weathered chair into an even more prominent position. "Just right."

"For what? The junk man?"

Lowering himself into the chair, Brad made himself comfortable before reaching out to grasp the shrunken head, tossing it between his hands as though it were a baseball.

"You're a sick man, Brad Holbrook." She pivoted and stalked out of the room.

As soon as she was out of sight, Brad gingerly returned the shrunken head to the table, not relishing contact with it despite his show for Kara. It had been a gift from a grateful client and represented a huge leap in growth for Holbrook Enterprises. Otherwise, he wouldn't have displayed the gruesome little treasure.

In moments, he heard the vacuum cleaner switch on. But almost as quickly, it clicked off. Kara backed out of the master bedroom with a look of renewed fury.

Brad hid his amusement. "I forgot to tell you. Erastus decided today to leave his suite of furniture in there. Said it held too many memories for him to take it off the ranch."

While each of them had purposely chosen another bedroom and left this one untouched, the significance was clear.

"Erastus really is going to hold us to this agreement, isn't he?"

"Well, he's not going to be inspecting our sleeping quarters," Brad said. Not that he would have minded that inclusion in the contract. It was hard to believe that he would be sharing close quarters for the next six months with this beautiful woman, pretending to be loving while knowing she was strictly hands-off.

She pushed back a heavy lock of golden hair. "I meant, we're really stuck with each other for at least six months."

Brad's male pride took a direct hit. Most of the women in his past hadn't considered themselves aggrieved to spend time with him. "I guess you could put it that way."

Kara sighed mightily. "I'm going to have to tell my mother. Until I read Erastus's clause, I figured she wouldn't have to know."

So that was it. A portion of his pride rebounded. "Invite her to dinner."

"Here?" Kara sounded horrified.

Narrowing his eyes, he studied her face. Somehow he hadn't envisioned her as such an old-fashioned girl. "Why not?"

"And just present our marriage a *fait accompli?*"

"People do elope," he reminded her.

"I can't imagine why."

Remembering the tacky chapel, he winced. "Maybe she'll think it's romantic."

"Ha! She knows I'm a practical person."

Brad's eyebrow lifted in disbelief. "You'd have a better time convincing someone of that who hadn't spent the past twenty-four hours with you."

"But, in my past . . ." Her voice trailed off, hating to admit her impulsive streak.

"You walked off your job and made sure you couldn't return. And you yanked out a very solid pension plan without knowing for sure you could invest it soon."

Irritated, she wished he wasn't so observant. "I didn't know you intended to parrot back everything I told you!"

"You didn't tell me all the details," Brad reminded her. "Erastus Jones pried them out of you."

Kara glared at him, but Brad didn't look perturbed. "He wanted to know why it was important for us to buy so quickly. I could hardly tell him that we were trying to take advantage of his mistake. That we were duping him into believing we were the happy couple he was looking for."

Brad shrugged. "I don't think we're doing him a disservice. We plan to enlarge the flock, make improvements. The ranch is in good hands."

Golden flecks swam in her green eyes as she fixed them on him. "But not the loving hands he intended. The place means so much to him. To me, it's freedom. But to Erastus . . ."

"He could have picked one of the other couples who might have been planning to bulldoze the ranch and build a shopping mall." Brad replaced the hammer in his toolbox. "Be practical, Kara. Erastus Jones is a romantic from another era."

Kara's expression dimmed into a cloud of disappointment. "I guess you're right. People really don't pledge themselves so wholly to another person anymore, do they?"

Staring at her, Brad felt a sudden, unexpected catch. He wished he could tell her that such commitment did still exist. But it wasn't that simple. "Kara, why don't you call your mother?"

His unexpected suggestion threw her. "Now?"

"Your old phone number won't work after today," he reminded her. "What if she tries to reach you?"

Feeling much like the spider in a very tangled web, Kara walked toward the phone, dreading the encounter. Especially since she'd been avoiding her mother since the elopement. Muriel had been duly suspicious, but Kara had purposely put her off, making one excuse after another to not talk to her.

Kara swallowed. How could she announce her marriage one day, then her annulment six months later?

But, as always, her mother was cheerful, delighted with the invitation to dinner. She was surprised by Kara's sudden purchase of the ranch, but not displeased. Of all people, Muriel Lawrence knew how badly her daughter had wanted to escape her job, to try her hand at a new, exciting venture.

The news that Kara was married was more surprising, however. Still, after a moment's pause, Muriel had even taken that well, saying she was looking forward to hearing all the details.

"She'll come for dinner tomorrow." Kara replaced the receiver reluctantly, hating to break the last link to sanity.

Brad was matter-of-fact. "Good. One down."

"Easy for you to say," she muttered.

"I'll be on my best manners. It's not like I'm going to stick my elbows in my soup or drink from the finger bowl."

"That'll be the least of my worries."

"And the worst?"

"Explaining why I married you."

MURIEL LAWRENCE WAS a lovely woman. It was easy to see where Kara got her fabulous looks. Although softer and in her late forties, Muriel still held the glow of ageless beauty. She could have passed for Kara's older sister.

Only her eyes were remarkably different. While Kara's flashed emerald fire, Muriel's piercing eyes were a deep blue. And farseeing, Brad noted, as her steady, perceptive gaze swept over him.

Kara, on the other hand, was a wreck. She had nearly burned dinner and the bright red welt on her finger was evidence of her run-in with some scalding water. A matching cut on her other hand had resulted from trying to chop the chives for the salad. Deciding that he might quickly become a widower, Brad had stepped in and finished the dinner while Kara whirled around the kitchen, cleaning invisible messes.

"Hey, calm down, she's just your mother," Brad soothed as Kara flew in from the living room, cheeks flushed, eyes a bit too bright.

"Why did I ever agree to this?" she wailed.

"Dinner or the marriage?"

"You realize that we have to put on a good show? I can't very well tell my own mother that I married you to get a *ranch!*"

Brad handed her three bowls of crisp, appetizing salad. "Instead, how about asking if she'd rather have blue cheese or Thousand Island for her salad." He placed a strategic hand on Kara's back and pushed gently. "Now, go."

They entered through the swinging door just seconds apart.

Muriel turned to them with a smile. "There you are. I was beginning to think I'd been deserted."

"Just a minor squall in the kitchen," Brad answered smoothly. "But all taken care of now."

Kara stood and stared blankly between them.

"Don't you want to serve the salad, dear?" Brad asked, refilling Muriel's glass.

"Oh, yes. Sure." Distracted, Kara handed her mother the three dishes of salad.

"I don't think I'm all that hungry," Muriel told her daughter with a twinkle, passing a dish to Brad and then one to Kara.

"Of course. Silly of me."

Muriel only laughed. "I think it's adorable. Imagine getting so caught up in a whirlwind romance that serving your mother dinner gets confusing." She turned a wide smile on Brad. "Tell me all about how you met. Kara's been so closemouthed, I didn't even know she'd met someone special." Her smile reached deep into her eyes as she said softly. "You must indeed be special to have swept Kara off her feet."

Indeed. Scrambling for believability, Brad took a healthy swallow of wine. He wished Muriel were the typical battle-ax mother-in-law typified in cartoons.

Instead, she seemed to be a genuine, caring person. The sort of woman he would have sought out as a friend. Not the sort he wished to crush with the truth of his arrangement with Kara. Muriel waited expectantly, an enchanting smile hovering on her lips.

"How could I resist her?" he finally blurted. "We bumped into each other in a crowded room. And I knew by the end of the day that I wanted to marry her."

Kara's mouth nearly dropped open at his variation of the truth.

But Brad had warmed up to the subject. "Since I own a charter aircraft company, it was easy to whisk Kara away to elope."

"And where did you go?" Muriel asked. "Kara hasn't told me a thing."

"To a lovely chapel in the desert."

Two identical sets of eyebrows rose at that statement.

Muriel turned to her daughter. "I didn't know you were fond of the desert."

Kara met Brad's eyes, that emerald fire rekindled. "It's a recent attachment."

"I do wish you would have had some of your friends and family with you," Muriel commented, not unkindly, but rather wistfully.

"The organist at the chapel thought we were a perfect couple," Brad added helpfully, wondering belatedly if Kara could do serious damage with the lightninglike warnings she was flashing at him.

"She was right, of course," Muriel agreed. "It's as though you're halves of a matched set. It never would have occurred to me before, since Kara's so independent. But it's as though you two just fit."

Brad and Kara stared at her, then at each other. This was getting uncanny.

"I can't wait to see your ring," Muriel commented.

Kara immediately stuck her hand behind her back. "Well, actually we got married in such a hurry that we didn't have a chance to get proper rings."

"Which I plan to take care of soon," Brad said. "We'll drape her in diamonds."

A small line wrinkled Muriel's forehead. "I never pictured Kara in anything so elaborate, but I'm sure you know best."

Kara managed to glare at him when Muriel glanced away.

"Actually we'll probably wait until our first anniversary," she fabricated nervously. "Right now I'd rather put that money into the ranch."

"Very sensible," Muriel agreed. "After all, commitment isn't about the outer trappings."

Kara and Brad mumbled simultaneously, then let the words trail away.

"Brad, tell me, how was Kara dressed during the ceremony?" Muriel asked, helping herself to the dressing.

"White lace and satin with a lot of bows," he improvised, thinking of his conservatively dressed bride. Hardly the description he could give her mother.

"Really." Muriel frowned. "How unlike her." Her eyes rested on Kara. "How did you happen to have an outfit like that on hand when you eloped?"

"I picked it out," Brad added, realizing he was digging an enormous hole, from which he might never be able to crawl out. "It was a surprise."

"I imagine it was, considering how Kara likes to dress," Muriel murmured. "But that's the fun of new love, discovering each other's tastes."

From the look on Kara's face it was evident that he was botching things badly. So she was strictly a wispy silk sort of girl. No wonder she was uncomfortable in the high-profile job she'd left. Power dressing in severe suits was undoubtedly mandatory.

"I can hardly wait to see the dress," Muriel continued.

"You can't. It's ruined," Brad improvised.

"That's terrible." Muriel lowered her glass to the table. "What happened?"

"I spilled wine on her . . ."

"I dumped spaghetti sauce all over . . ."

Their mismatched stories came out simultaneously as Muriel glanced between them with a look of confusion. "Then I guess it must be ruined. That's too bad. I brought my camera to take a few pictures. I was hoping to get one of Kara in her dress."

"It's still at the cleaners. . . ."

"I threw it out. . . ."

Muriel couldn't disguise the baffled look that covered her face.

Brad cleared his throat. "I meant to tell you, Kara. The cleaners said it was a total disaster so I threw it away. I'd hoped to buy another dress and replace it before you knew." He could feel the sweat beading on his brow. While he wasn't Mr. Joe All-American, he wasn't generally an out-and-out liar, either.

"That's all right. A duplicate would never be the same as the original, but it was sweet of you to think of it." Kara was looking positively feverish as she spoke, Brad decided. Any more of this confusion and she would probably lose her tenuous grip on calmness.

"Kara's right. That was a thoughtful gesture. I'm just sorry I spoke up and ruined your surprise." Distress coated Muriel's words.

"Better that you did," Brad replied. "If I'd tricked her and she found out later, well . . ."

"Mother, I've made pasta." Desperation edged Kara's words.

"That's nice, dear." Muriel glanced at her daughter with a doting expression. "I suppose Brad was delighted to find out that you're a gourmet cook."

At least he wouldn't starve. Deciding silence might be the best part of valor, he smiled at his new mother-in-law.

It soon became clear that Kara was trying to rush the dinner as quickly as possible. If he'd bungled his part, she wasn't doing much better. Such transparent motives wouldn't go unnoticed for long.

But Muriel was right. Kara was an excellent cook. Even when she was tremendously nervous.

"This is delicious," Brad said with appreciation.

"Thanks," she muttered, still distracted.

"Did Kara mention that she tried to impress her first boyfriend with her cooking?" Muriel took some of the shrimp and asparagus sauce and ladled it over her fettucini.

Brad hid his smile with an effort. This dinner could prove interesting. Especially since Kara looked like a bug under a microscope. A very uncomfortable bug.

"No, I don't believe she did." He purposely ignored Kara's glare.

"She wanted a theme for the evening and so she decided it would be color. She cooked a beautiful pasta dinner, but unfortunately the color she chose for the evening was blue. Tinted the noodles blue, the cream sauce, and the cauliflower. It's hard to work up an appetite when everything's blue." Muriel shook her head. "Even the cheesecake, which she topped with blueberries, of course. Poor boy, he was absolutely green."

"Which wasn't part of the theme?" Brad queried politely, with a devilish gleam in his expression.

Muriel laughed. "Exactly. Kara was mortified, but it really was amusing. Her father and I tried to tell her that Alfred Hitchcock had made the same mistake at an infamous Hollywood buffet, but Kara would have none of it. Thought her social life was ruined forever."

"But she recovered?" he asked, enjoying the subtle needling.

"I should say so. Every boy in school wanted to take her out the very next week."

"Oh?"

Muriel grinned. "Seemed they all had an assignment to produce mold for science. I guess they thought Kara had cornered the market."

"Mother!"

"Oops, guess I went too far." Muriel turned a conspiratorial smile toward Brad. "I can tell by the tone she's using."

"I'd rather we didn't trot out every embarrassing episode from my adolescence," Kara responded stiffly.

"Surely that wasn't all," Brad said helpfully.

Kara only glared.

Muriel broke the tension. "Could I have a tour of your home? I couldn't possibly eat any dessert for a while. That way I won't have to whip out photos of Kara as a baby on a bearskin rug.''

Kara rose to her feet rapidly, not sure if her mother was only teasing. "Certainly. I'll show you around."

"I'll clear," Brad offered.

"What a thoughtful man you've married," Muriel said as Kara led her into the den, study and then through the entry hall, which led back to the dining room.

"Oh... yes." It was difficult to disagree since that was the impression Kara had wanted to establish, although she was ready to wring Brad's neck. *Satin and lace? With bows?* Where had that come from? And the gruesome memories from her childhood. It seemed her mother had found a ready ally in Brad. Their matching grins would have been amusing if she hadn't been the target of their ribbing.

"Your furniture seems to blend together well," Muriel commented as they reentered the dining room.

"Yeah, right," Brad mocked.

"Sure," Kara muttered at the same time.

"Much like you two."

Kara contained a gasp.

"I really like the place," Muriel continued. "I think you've made an excellent choice. You're lucky it was available so quickly after you married."

The understatement of the century.

They moved through the rooms. Heading toward the hall housing the bedrooms, Kara's footsteps dragged.

As they paused at the entrance of the master suite, Muriel again showed her enthusiasm. "Oh, darling. This is wonderful. So old-fashioned and romantic. What a beautiful room for you both."

Uncomfortably Kara stared at the intimate furnishings. The antique four-poster bed was the focal point of the room, along with an enchanting window seat that faced a huge trailing oak tree outside.

"Would you like to see the rest of house, Mom?"

"Certainly."

They reached the next bedroom, which was furnished with Kara's things from her apartment. Realizing her mistake too late, she tried to breeze by the room.

"What's this, Kara?" Her mother surveyed the familiar furniture, and recognition dawned. "Oh, I see. You've used your old bedroom furniture from your apartment in the guest room."

"Sure . . . I mean, yes. That's what I did."

When they moved on to the next room, Kara nearly groaned aloud. This was the room Brad had chosen. Muriel studied the contents.

"If I'm not mistaken, you've done the same thing with Brad's bachelor furniture."

Kara smiled weakly, wondering if she'd be struck dead for lying so blatantly to her mother. "It seemed like the thing to do."

"How clever. That way you both have something from your prior lives. But, wisely you've chosen something fresh and different for your new start together. Of course, when the children come, you'll probably want to turn one of these rooms into a nursery."

Kara couldn't contain the choking cough that sent her into a spasm.

Muriel patted her on the back. "Are you all right? Something must have gone down the wrong pipe."

Boy, had it ever.

As they returned to the den, lightning flashed through the huge picture window, accompanied by a loud crack of thunder. Immediately thick sheets of rain splattered against the windows. As though huge buckets had been overturned, the water fell like a dense curtain.

"Did you hear anything about a storm?" Kara asked Brad as she stared in consternation out the window. Houston was famous for its sudden storms and subsequent flooding. Dry one moment, the streets leading to Houston could be impassable within minutes.

Brad flipped the television on. A local newscaster bemoaned the latest flood warning.

"Oh, dear," Muriel murmured. "It looks like I'm going to be stranded."

Kara's throat grew dry as she dared a glance at Brad. "Stranded?"

Ignoring Kara, he glanced in concern at Muriel. "You can't go out in this." His eyes shifted to meet Kara's. "One wrong turn and she could be sliding off the road into a creek or a river."

"Which you can't see when the flooding starts," Kara agreed dismally. Too many people had met an unfortunate end in just that way—drowned by overflowing creeks on roads that had been dry only hours earlier. Kara certainly didn't want to send her mother into a dangerous situation, but what in the world were they going to do with her?

The television newscaster now warned motorists to seek shelter and stay off the roads, some of which were already flooded.

Muriel looked anxious. "I'm glad you had the foresight to set up guest rooms, dear. I hate to overstay my welcome, particularly on your honeymoon, but I am a little reluctant to drive in this."

Kara met Brad's eyes in alarm. *Honeymoon!*

The newscaster chose that moment to resound the flood warning, which now flashed intermittently across the screen.

"Guest room?" Brad mouthed to Kara while Muriel's attention was diverted by the television.

"Fortunately, I showed Mom the two guest rooms we'd set up with the old furniture from our apartments," Kara said brightly, managing to maintain an expression that hovered between desperation and pleading.

It took him a minute, but he got it. "Good. She can have her pick...." His voice trailed off as he saw Kara trying to pantomime a new message. She tugged at her clothes and pointed in the direction of the bedrooms, but he couldn't decipher the latest message.

Kara's voice was frantically bright. "I'll just go freshen up your room, Mom."

Muriel waved her hands in dismissal. "What's to freshen? You just moved here. I doubt you've given the dust time to settle."

"Sheets!" Kara practically shouted. "There aren't any sheets on the bed." She met Brad's eyes as Muriel swung back around. "And I'm sure you won't know which of the *dresser drawers* they're stored in."

Comprehension dawned in Brad's eyes. Their clothes were stored in those dresser drawers. Muriel would wonder why. Fortunately everything hadn't been unpacked, but still...

"I think Brad could use some help clearing the dishes, Mom, and I have to...check on the...birds. Yes, the birds," she repeated, grasping at the excuse.

"Wouldn't that be more in Brad's area of expertise?" Muriel questioned innocently.

"Well, yes. Normally." Kara tried not to sound as rattled as she felt. "But we just installed a new type of thermostat and I've been reading up on it, so I'd be the one to check on it."

"Won't you get all wet in the storm?"

"Uh, no," Kara improvised. "The thermostat's on the service porch out of the weather. We purposely installed a remote control device in case of storms." She continued smiling even though Brad rolled his eyes in disbelief at this whopper. "And then I'll get your room ready, Mom."

Muriel glanced at her daughter in admiration. "You're really determined about this business. I've never known you to be the least bit mechanical before."

"Well, it's amazing what challenging circumstances can do for you."

Behind Muriel's back, Brad's widened eyes telegraphed a message of his own. Through gritted teeth he mouthed *Hurry!* Glancing at the dining room table, Kara belatedly realized why. Brad had already been clearing the dishes and little remained of their dinner.

"I'll just be a minute," Kara promised as she backed out of the room.

As soon as she was clear of their line of vision, Kara dashed into her bedroom at the end of the hall. She knew what she'd unpacked and she could be sure to retrieve everything. Throwing open dresser drawers, she scooped up an armful of clothes and dashed into the master suite. Looking around frantically, she knew she couldn't just dump the mess in the middle of the room. She ripped open the closet door and threw the pile inside.

Flying out of the master bedroom, she saw Brad wave frantically as he tried to keep Muriel from turning around. Kara darted out of sight as she heard Brad suggest that Muriel help him with something in the kitchen. Praying her mother would agree, Kara dashed back to her room and emptied another drawer. A glance at the perfume on the dresser top had her reaching for those items, as well. She froze as voices grew closer to the room.

"Muriel, I know you were headed for bed, but I'd really like your help with the dessert. It was supposed to be a surprise for Kara, but I'm all thumbs when it comes to cooking. Of course, if you're too tired..."

"How sweet. Of course, I'll help. I noticed that Kara wasn't eating much. Maybe this will perk up her appetite."

Their voices faded and Kara released a pent-up breath. That was a close call.

In two more quick trips, Kara had the dresser cleared out.

"I could have sworn I bought the chocolate," Brad was saying.

"It was a good idea, maybe next time when you've got all the ingredients," Muriel replied.

The voices were coming closer and Kara held her breath.

"Why don't we sit in the living room?" Brad suggested. "Kara wants to make the room extra nice."

"But there's no need to fuss," Muriel protested.

"You know how new brides are," Brad countered, sounding strained at the pretense.

Kara grabbed the few clothes she'd hung in the closet. Fortunately the rest of them were in the boxes still stored in the trailer. Glancing around the room, Kara made sure she'd left no clues behind.

She reentered the living room, pasting on a bright smile. "Your room's all set."

Brad rose, the relief on his face clear. "I think I'll make some coffee. It may be a long...I mean cold evening."

"I really am tired. I think I'll skip the coffee and turn in," Muriel said, getting to her feet.

"But it's early," Kara protested.

Her mother's glance fell meaningfully between Kara and Brad. "Not really. I'll see you two in the morning. Fortunately, I sleep like a rock."

"Since when?" Kara muttered.

But her mother only smiled. "Oh, I would like to snap a quick picture if I could." Muriel reached into her purse and produced a camera. After switching on the flash, she glanced at them expectantly. "How about a romantic pose?" Her smile twinkled. "I'll pretend they're wedding photos."

Brad moved forward, Kara saw gratefully. It was a good thing, since her own legs seemed suddenly paralyzed. He draped a casual arm around her and smiled.

"Closer," Muriel instructed as she focused the camera.

Brad angled his head deliberately close to Kara's, looking as though as he were trailing a kiss near her earlobe. "Smile, dammit, or the jig's going to be up."

Complying, Kara tried not to focus on the sensations as Brad's arm rested on her shoulders, their bodies close together, his warm breath sending unexpected goose bumps where it touched.

"That'll do it. Next time I'm here we'll have to shoot a whole roll of film."

"Great," Kara and Brad murmured simultaneously. Startled eyes met. She was growing uneasy with their matching reactions.

"You sure you don't want some coffee, Mom?" Perhaps she could talk her mother into staving off the inevitable awhile longer.

"Absolutely. Besides, I love to sleep to the sound of pouring rain."

It took only a few minutes to settle her mother into the room Kara had chosen for her. Since her mother was the same size, it was easy to outfit her with a gown and robe. Refusing to be fussed over, Muriel waved Kara away quickly.

Feeling as though she were walking to her own execution, Kara reluctantly returned to the den. Brad had turned off the television. The stereo played softly. From her viewpoint, she could see only the back of his head, the slope of his broad shoulders. In front of him on the table, she could see that instead of coffee, he had poured two glasses of wine.

Immediately she froze.

If he planned to take advantage of the situation, she would kill him. Half-expecting to see his shirt unbuttoned, his smile loose and knowing, she stormed around the front of the couch and halted.

Lying on the couch next to him was a spray of wild summer roses, ones that grew just outside the back porch. He must have clipped them from the trellis, since they were barely moist, protected from the driving rain. The pale magenta blossoms perfumed the air.

Her eyes widened as she took in the scene, her mind clicking furiously as she tried to decide just what tack he was taking. The fact that she was attracted to him made her all that much more suspicious.

Brad's smile was noncommittal. "I figured you'd had about all you could take for one evening. I'm not sure how I'd feel if my mother had just tripped through some of my most embarrassing moments. Truce?"

Cautiously she took a seat on the couch, wondering what he was up to now.

He held out a single flower blossom. "Maybe now we can have time for the wine and roses we skipped in Vegas."

Unexpectedly her throat closed as her heart thawed, even some of the places she had kept carefully barricaded for years. Darn the man. And did he have to look so handsome in the declining light?

"Wine?" he asked.

She nodded and he handed her a glass of chardonnay.

"You can relax. I'm not going to leap off the couch and ravish you." His smile grew slightly wider, one full lip edging upward in amusement.

Cautiously she sipped her wine until his ebony eyes darkened to an impossible hue as he spoke. "Even though I do get to sleep with you tonight."

Chapter Four

"That's not funny," she hissed.

"If you could see your face, you'd think so."

"I can't help it if my mother's staying here. I didn't think you were the sort to take advantage of the situation."

"I can sleep in the spare room," Brad offered, reaching for his wineglass. "Or in the study. It has a decent couch that makes into a bed."

"Fine. And then she'll think something's wrong."

He refilled her glass. "This will relax you."

"Great."

"Don't you trust me?"

"Not particularly."

He frowned. "Why not?"

"Because, despite this charade, I don't know you. You are a complete stranger."

"That you're married to," he reminded her.

"Thanks to you. And now I'm lying to my mother, putting on a pretense, and to top it off, I don't have any place to sleep."

He replaced his wineglass on the table. "Don't sweat it. It's a big room." His voice grew dry. "And I'll try to restrain myself."

Reluctantly she met his eyes and realized she had been carrying on too much. He was right. There was no reason why they couldn't share a room for one night. With all the suddenness and tension of the past few days, she was prickly and overly sensitive.

The wine was beginning to relax her a bit, along with the music and the aroma of the flowers. But, after a half hour had passed, she realized she couldn't sit all night on the sofa. Slowly she acknowledged that they would have to retire.

Feeling awkward, she entered the master suite, knowing he was only a few steps behind. It really was a beautiful room. And, unfortunately, both romantic and intimate. Trying to ignore both of those features, she reached for the nightgown she had filched from her own room and froze.

Brad's gaze was fastened on her, noting the movement. Eyes of granite darkened at the same time. Like obsidian shadows, they devoured her. Breath short, she stared at him.

Tall, muscular, he seemed to dominate the suddenly diminished space in the bedroom. Did he have to be such a perfect male specimen? Aware of their disturbing proximity, she closed her hand over the gown and tried to disguise the fragile bit of silk.

But he turned away. Taking the opportunity, she escaped down the hall, fleeing toward the safety of the spare bedroom. Seeing her mother emerge from the bathroom, Kara managed a smile.

"I was just headed there next." Kara veered away from the bedroom and toward the bath.

"The rain's still coming down," her mother commented. "Sounds like it will storm all night."

"That's what I'm afraid of," Kara muttered.

"At least you won't have to be alone for the storm."

Kara had always hated the lightning. And her poor mother was completely alone in the storm. As she had been for almost ten years. Protectiveness surged forward as it had since her mother had been abruptly widowed.

But Muriel handed her a gift wrapped box.

"What's this?" Kara asked.

"Just a little something for you." Muriel's expression brightened. "Open it."

Pulling off the ribbon and opening the box, Kara found a nightgown nestled among the tissue. Holding it up, she realized it was an incredibly extravagant present. "Mom, it's..." She couldn't tell her the truth. "It's beautiful."

"You'll make it beautiful, darling."

Kara started to demur but Muriel interrupted. "I want to see it on you."

"But—"

"I couldn't be part of the wedding, but this...well, I wanted to do this for you."

Weakly Kara tried to protest as she stared in dismay at the folds of diaphanous material. "But—"

"Please, Kara."

Reluctantly Kara entered the bathroom and donned the alluring garment. Staring into the mirror, Kara realized it was even worse than she'd thought. Self-consciously she put one hand over the rather large expanse of flesh that the neckline exposed. The formfitting gown didn't leave much to the imagination. She could just picture Brad's reaction if she strolled back into the bedroom, dressed so sensuously.

Taking a breath, Kara opened the door. "It's really lovely."

Muriel beamed, then leaned forward to fluff Kara's hair. "You need a bit of lipstick, dear." Not waiting for Kara, Muriel reached into the pocket of her robe and brought out a tube.

"Just happened to have that in your pocket, Mom?"

"I was hoping to run into you before bedtime," she admitted without a shade of repentance. Stepping back, Muriel examined Kara's makeup and then returned the lipstick to her pocket. In seconds, she whipped out perfume, as well.

"Mom!"

But she'd already been spritzed. The sensual fragrance lingered in the air and Kara could have groaned out loud. If her mother only knew the truth! But that wasn't a possibility. Muriel's own loveless match had been painful. So much that she'd never even considered remarrying after being widowed at a young age. How was Kara going to confess that she, too, had plunged into a marriage without love?

Muriel kissed Kara's cheek, sparkling blue eyes radiant as her gaze lingered on her daughter's face. "I can't tell you how good it makes me feel to know you're settled and happy."

Kara hugged her back. "Sleep well, Mom."

But Muriel wasn't budging. "You go on to bed. I'll be fine."

"But—"

"I think we've let your young man wait long enough as it is."

Kara had hoped to escape back into the bathroom and change so that Brad wouldn't see her in the gown, but it was clear that Muriel wasn't moving.

She retraced her steps to the master suite. At the door she hesitated. Turning, she met her mother's fond glance. Muriel waved and weakly Kara returned the gesture. Apparently there would be no reprieve.

Firming her shoulders, Kara reentered the bedroom awkwardly. "Bath's free."

He inclined his head toward the master bath. "So's this one."

Apparently he wasn't having any of it. He knew she had resorted to escape. Feeling foolish, she fingered the delicate lace at the deep neckline of her gown. Seeing his eyes follow the motion, she stopped abruptly. "My mother likes you."

"I like her."

Kara laughed, a small, strained sound. "You're not supposed to. In normal marriages, husbands can't stand their mothers-in-law."

"But this isn't a normal marriage, is it, Kara?"

The tension was thick, impenetrable. Swallowing the impossibly large lump in her throat, she shook her head. "No, I don't suppose it is."

She watched as his eyes traveled over her neck and arms, bared by the silken gown. The alluring gown, accompanied by the fact that it was the sole garment she wore, made her incredibly nervous. She crossed her arms in front of her in a protective fashion, unknowingly pulling the fabric even tighter across her breasts. "Look, just so you know. This gown wasn't my idea."

A light flashed in his eyes and the dent in his chin deepened. "You usually wear steel-belted pajamas?"

She flushed. "My mother insisted. It was a gift."

His look was long and languorous, warming her in an unexpected, unwanted way. "She has good taste."

Kara tried to look at everything except him since he was clad only in very brief boxers. Suspecting she'd barged in on him while changing, she kept her gaze focused on a point behind him, rather than on the fleshy expanse of muscular arms and legs and the matted steel of his torso. It was like an overdose of golden, tanned skin and muscle. A very heady overdose. "In some things," she muttered.

His lips twitched as though knowing why she didn't look at him. "Hope she's got a trunk full of negligees along with her."

Wishing for her old flannel robe, Kara pulled the flimsy fabric closer together, wondering why the room again suddenly seemed smaller. It was as though Brad's presence, his very revealing, nerve-racking presence dominated and filled the entire bedroom. Feeling tongue-tied and awkward, she waited for Brad to put on some more clothing. "She's not a saleslady for Victoria's Secret."

His gaze deepened as one eyebrow arched. "Oh, so it was really your idea all along?"

"Very funny. I have better things to do than seduce you."

Those deeply black eyes darkened even further. "Pity."

She swallowed, unable to form an intelligent reply.

Then he gestured around the room. "There aren't many choices in here."

Her ears rang, and her overaccelerated pulse was doing serious damage to her ability to concentrate. But his words...was he changing tactics again? "Excuse me?"

Brad pointed to the bed, a solitary vanity chair and the window seat. "Doesn't look like Erastus and Sarah spent much time sleeping apart."

Managing to avoid looking at him, Kara glanced around, realizing he was right. The small metal vanity chair would be a torture rack and the window seat was too short to completely recline. The polished hardwood floor wasn't a likely alternative, either.

Unwillingly her eyes traveled to the four-postered bed. "This is silly. I'm sure we can share a bed without . . . without . . ."

"Agreed."

Her brow lifted in question at his quick consensus.

"Otherwise, I'd have to offer to sleep on the floor, and my bones are already protesting that option."

Feeling absurdly self-conscious, Kara looked at the bed and then away again. "With all the rain, do you think we should check on the ostriches?"

"The pens are built at the top of an incline, remember? In case of floods?"

"Right. I just forgot." *Wasn't there another excuse she could think of? One that would occupy the rest of the hours until dawn?*

"I've got to get some sleep," Brad announced.

While she watched spellbound, the lamplight shone sinuously over his skin and Kara felt her mouth go dry.

"You going to stand there all night?"

As she swallowed to regain her equilibrium, Brad crawled into the bed, still clad in the brief underwear. Irritation kicked in. "Aren't you going to put on some pajamas?"

He met her eyes without missing a beat. "It's this or nothing, babe."

"You could make an exception," she retorted.

He reached for the blanket, shrugging impressive shoulders. "Whatever you say. It can be nothing."

Guessing he wasn't bluffing, she held up one hand. "Since my mother's in the next room, you win. For tonight."

He lifted one eyebrow. "We'll see about that."

Unwilling to have her mother overhear any arguing, Kara swallowed a testy reply. But she stood uncertainly next to the bed, unwilling to share the narrow space with him.

"Get in," he barked suddenly. "I'm not going to attack."

Trying to look confident and assured, Kara gingerly lowered herself to the bed and, taking a deep breath, scooted under the covers. Her bravado collapsed when she felt the long, hard length of Brad's body close to hers. Jerking away, she scuttled toward the edge.

His exasperated sigh echoed in the room. "Look. This is awkward. Damned awkward." Brad ran a hand through already disheveled hair. "Why don't we just try to get some sleep. After the past few days, I'll sleep like the dead."

BUT HE DIDN'T. Instead Brad heard the rustle of the bed linens as Kara moved restlessly. Hours had passed, but he couldn't sleep. The fragrance of her perfume sifted through the air. Aware that only a foot of space separated them, Brad found himself lying in a rigidly controlled pose, afraid to move. Afraid that otherwise he would seek out that golden hair, that intriguing face, that lean, supine body.

A body, his relentless mind repeated, that belonged to his wife. Their mock marriage plans had never included sharing a bed. And now that they did, he was even more aware of the woman at his side.

Rain still fell in fat, noisy drops, blanketing the house in a protective layer from the howling wind. But all Brad could think of was the way Kara's mouth had felt under his when they had sealed their marriage vows. All soft, warm and yielding. As though if the ceremony had been real, the evening would have ended very differently.

Delicate lace curtains covered the windows, allowing the moonlight to illuminate the room. His gaze traveled over the unfamiliar furnishings. It was easy to imagine Erastus and his bride here. More difficult to imagine what he was doing here.

Turning his head slightly, Brad watched as moonbeams speared the golden swath of silken hair covering the pillow next to his. If he reached out ever so slightly, he could trace her profile, investigate those curves her gown hinted at. The arch of her hip beckoned seductively, the folds of her gown settling against the curving valley of her waist. If he reached out, he could touch the lush breasts merely a hand's span away. He wondered if the sexy gown had really been a gift from her mother. Or could it be that Kara only owned gowns designed to drive a man mad?

Biting back a sharp stab of arousal, he wondered if he would awaken her if he rose and left the delicious torment of the bed. He listened for a moment, his suspicions suddenly alerted. The even breathing beside him made Brad wonder if she was actually asleep.

"Kara?"

Her response was immediate. "Yes?"

So she wasn't asleep, either.

"You're still awake."

Her hands fluttered against the sheet. "I was going to tell you—"

A thunderous crash reverberated through the house.

The sound sent them both scrambling upward and out of the bed.

"What was that?" Kara shrieked, disoriented.

But Brad was already running, fear and adrenaline giving him speed. The sound had come from down the hall. Where Muriel slept.

Kara was on his heels as he skidded to a halt. An enormous tree trunk complete with wet, dripping leaves filled the hall, pushing its huge girth through the bathroom and bedrooms.

"Mom!" Kara breathed, her eyes glistening with unshed tears, her voice a croak of horror.

Muriel's door ripped open at that moment. Although white as a sheet, she looked unharmed. Her voice was shaky. "Some storm, huh?"

"Are you all right?" Brad asked, shoving Kara behind him and climbing over the tree trunk. In seconds he was at Muriel's side.

"I'm fine. If that tree had fallen any closer, I'd be spitting toothpicks, though."

Brad peered into the room behind her. Only a portion of the room was untouched. The remainder was crushed beneath the tree trunk. The angle at which it had fallen had spared Muriel by inches. No wonder she looked like a ghost. From all appearances, they'd just lost the rest of the rooms off the hall. His and Kara's bedrooms were destroyed along with almost everything from their prior lives.

Brad helped Muriel over the tree trunk that now decorated the house.

"Well, dear. You certainly know how to keep the evening lively," Muriel managed to say as Kara hugged her.

"I think we could all use that coffee now," Brad stated.

Kara stared down the hall at the destruction and then back at him. The space of their lodgings had just been reduced significantly. By her count, they now had one bedroom.

SUNLIGHT DAPPLED OVER the rain-soaked grass. Bright, warm and radiant, it seemed as though no storm had ever passed their way. But water-filled ditches offered proof that the storm had been very real. Along with a crushed section of the ranch house that looked as though it had been hit by a SCUD missile.

"I'm sure your insurance will cover the damage," Muriel comforted as she poured three glasses of juice in addition to the bracing cups of coffee.

"What a start," Kara muttered, tired after the sleepless night. None of them had felt like trying to sleep after the crash. Instead they'd consumed endless cups of coffee and talked through the remaining hours of darkness.

"I'll check on the birds," Brad said, excusing himself.

Muriel replaced the pitcher of juice. "The news report said that my part of town was hit hard. Do you mind if I call and check on my house?"

"Of course not, Mom."

Kara stared out the bay window as she heard the quiet sounds of her mother talking on the phone. Only when Muriel's voice filled with distress did Kara visibly eavesdrop, trying to discover what was wrong.

Muriel replaced the receiver, her hand lingering on the phone before turning to face her daughter.

"Mom, what is it?"

Brad reentered the kitchen, his gaze darting between the two distraught women.

"My house. It's flooded." Muriel's voice caught for a moment before she steadied it. "Apparently the walls are completely washed out."

"Oh no!" Kara jumped from the table to comfort her mother.

Muriel accepted her hug. "What hurts most are the mementos I can't replace."

"Maybe everything's not ruined, Mom."

Strain edged Muriel's face. "I hope not. But, of course, I also don't have any place to stay."

"You'll stay here," Kara insisted.

"I can't. You're newlyweds. One night was an imposition. Any more would be—"

"Kara's right. You'll stay with us." Brad's firm voice interrupted them both, triggering a mixed set of expressions. Relief, consternation and gratitude crowded across Kara's face.

A loud rap on the back door startled them all.

"What now?" Brad muttered as he opened the door.

"Just thought I'd check for bodies, dead or alive," Chuck greeted him. "That's one big hole in your house."

Brad waved toward the women. "As you can see, we're all in one piece. Want some coffee?"

"Sure. Morning, Kara." Chuck's expression changed as his gaze traveled from Kara to her mother.

He straightened up, pulling his tall frame into an alert position as he addressed Muriel. "Hello."

Brad made the introductions, noting the interest on Chuck's face as he studied Muriel. Just what he needed. His devil-may-care pilot interested in his mother-in-law. More complications they certainly could do without.

Muriel's hand rested a tad longer than necessary in Chuck's grip. Brad could have groaned aloud. While he thought the world of his chief pilot and friend, Brad knew it would be difficult enough to carry out this farce without adding the extra deception of more people to convince. No, he needed to extinguish this bud of interest immediately.

"Any damage at the hangar?" he asked Chuck.

"Huh?" Chuck dragged his gaze away from Muriel. "Nah. We moved all the airplanes inside before the wind picked up."

"Good, the last thing we need is more damage."

"Right." Chuck took the seat next to Muriel as Kara produced an extra mug. He focused his attention on Muriel, his eyes traveling over her in undisguised interest. "Did you get stuck out here during the storm?"

"I'm afraid so," Muriel replied, a soft smile enveloping the graceful lines of her face, replacing the earlier strain.

"She was sleeping where the tree crashed," Kara added, still shaken by the incident.

"You all right?" Chuck asked, taking the opportunity to let his gaze sweep over Muriel again.

She blushed, a charming, almost entrancing spectacle. Pale rose tinged her cheeks as she met his concerned eyes. "I'm like a cat. And fortunately I still have several of my lives left."

Obviously intrigued, Chuck inclined his head toward Muriel. "I'm glad of that. Brad didn't tell me the side benefits of his marriage included you."

Muriel laughed, a silvery tinkling sound.

Brad exchanged a glance with Kara, who looked startled at her mother's interchange with Chuck.

"Don't you need to be checking in at the airport?" Brad asked, knowing that short of hauling Chuck out of his chair, he was going to be difficult to dislodge.

"Nope. I'm off today."

"It's a beautiful day for it," Muriel commented, picking up her own mug of coffee.

"But we've got a lot of cleaning to do, calling the insurance company, things like that," Brad hinted broadly to his friend.

Momentarily diverted, Chuck narrowed his gaze on Brad and Kara. "Gee, you two aren't acting like the lovebirds I'm used to."

Immediately defensive, aware that his own hints had apparently fallen far short of subtle, Brad stared pointedly at Chuck. "What do you mean?"

"Usually you can't keep your hands off each other," Chuck replied, a wicked light in his eyes.

"I imagine they've been restraining themselves since I'm here," Muriel offered.

"Nah," Chuck continued his needling. "Don't tell me you've had a lovers' quarrel?"

Brad gritted his teeth. "Hardly any of your concern now, is it?"

Muriel's brow puckered into a frown. "I hope my being here hasn't caused a problem."

"Of course not, Mom." Kara glared at Brad and then Chuck. "We loved having you here."

"You're not acting like it." Chuck's bright blue eyes fairly twinkled with amusement.

Brad slipped an arm around Kara's waist. "Satisfied?"

But Chuck, now thoroughly relishing his role as devil's advocate, shook his head. "Oh, I don't think so."

Kara took Brad's hand in hers. "See? All happy on the honeymoon home front."

Chuck glanced at Muriel in mock concern. "Not even a kiss? What do you think? Trouble in paradise?"

Wishing he could get his hands around Chuck's neck, Brad stared at the varying expressions on the faces of the three other people in the room.

Muriel's face filled with concern. Chuck smirked, his eyes dancing with unrepentant deviltry. And Kara looked as though she wanted to kill him.

Muriel turned away from Chuck to stare at her daughter and new son-in-law. "I think I'm the problem. They don't need me in their way."

"That's not—"

"No, Mom—"

Brad and Kara broke off their simultaneous protest as Muriel rose to her feet. "I insist. I'm leaving right now. I'll find a hotel. There's nothing honeymooners need less than a mother-in-law. Thanks for a truly *interesting* evening." She smiled, a dimple flashing in her cheek. "Maybe next time we could just do videos, instead of destroying the house."

"Hotel? Nothing doing, Mom."

"Why does she need a hotel?" Chuck asked, obviously baffled.

"Because her house flooded last night and we just talked her into staying here," Brad warned him.

"Oh, hell, I was just kidding around." Chuck ignored the others as he gazed directly at Muriel, trying to smooth things over. "Don't mind what I said. Why don't I take you to your house to check things out? Brad and Kara have their hands full here."

Muriel hesitated, obviously torn. "I really should find a hotel and get out of their way. The extra bedrooms have been ruined—"

"The study has a foldout couch and there's plenty of room, Mom."

"Please, Muriel, we insist," Brad added quietly, the conviction in his voice leaving little room for argument.

Looking between them, her gaze lingering on her new son-in-law, Muriel made up her mind. "If you're sure—"

"They are," Chuck said. "Now, why don't I drive you to your house?"

"I can drive myself."

"It's not a sight you should tackle alone," Chuck insisted.

Muriel saw the interest etched across his face and gave in to a long-buried feminine impulse. One that said she'd like to be cosseted and protected. "I *would* like to see if I can salvage anything." She glanced pointedly at her daughter. "And I'm not dragging Kara away today. She has a husband who needs her."

Kara opened her mouth to protest, but Muriel held up her hand. "No arguing or I won't stay here."

Kara could only smile rigidly, still feeling Brad's arm around her, remembering the tense moments they'd shared the night before.

Chuck saw his opportunity and ushered Muriel outside. Together they walked to his truck as Brad and Kara watched from the doorway, his arm still looped around her waist. Brad lifted a hand to wave goodbye, but Chuck wasn't through.

"I thought you two were going to kiss and make up."

Brad stared down at the face so close to his own. Translucent skin glowed in the morning sun. Incredible emerald eyes swam with gold flecks, reminding him of rich, marbleized jade. Except that, unlike any cold gem, Kara's eyes were warm. Devastatingly so.

Full, moist lips trembled as he angled his head toward her. It was as though the anticipation alone made her shiver. Sliding his tongue along the edge of her mouth, he felt her sigh as she opened her lips and accepted his kiss.

Rocked by the sensation, Brad deepened the kiss beyond what he intended. Forgetting his audience, he pulled her body against his, savoring soft against hard. The press of her breasts pushed into his chest, which was abraded by the buttons closing their shirts. He felt the curve of her legs molded against his longer ones.

His hand reached to cup the alluring curve of her snug bottom, when a sound pierced his consciousness.

"Whew, boss! You win," Chuck hooted. "We believe you!"

Kara and Brad jerked apart and turned startled faces toward Muriel and Chuck. Met by matching grins, they could only smile weakly as the truck pulled out of the driveway, leaving behind a swirl of up-raised dust. And another brewing storm.

Chapter Five

"What do you mean *you don't know?*" Brad squared off and stared at Kara in growing disbelief.

Prickly ever since their kiss, she stubbornly stood her ground. "I'm not the only one responsible here."

"But you're the one who spouted off that you knew so much about the ostrich business—your lifelong dream."

"Freedom's been my lifelong dream," she corrected him huffily. "And I didn't expect to be roped into buying a ranch in such a rush."

"You *said* your time was running out," Brad reminded her.

"It was. But how'd I know you'd go and order new birds right away? Before we'd checked the corrals?"

"We agreed that we wanted to up the profit. How'd I know you were bluffing about how much you really knew about ostriches?"

"I wasn't," she hotly denied. "I've read enough books on ostriches to practically be an expert!"

"Books?" His face fell into disbelieving lines as his voice rose. "You think you're going to run a ranch based on books? What're you going to do? Tell the birds to stand still while you turn the page?"

Anger glinted from moss-colored eyes. "I didn't see you volunteering the fact that you're a complete greenhorn. When were you going to reveal that little gem? After you'd killed more of the flock by forgetting to turn on the heat in the incubators?" She turned and pointed at the unwanted load of new stock. "I'm surprised you managed to order the right species!"

The driver tooted his horn, disturbing their battle. Both heads jerked in the direction of the truck containing their new stock. "I ain't got all day. You acceptin' delivery or not?"

A muscle twitched in Brad's cheek. "We're accepting it all right."

"Driver, I'll take charge," Kara interrupted. She'd show Brad she knew what she was doing.

The driver hollered back at her. "How're you gonna unload these birds?"

"Aren't you going to do that?" she asked in surprise.

"No way, lady. My job's to drive 'em here. Nobody said nothing about unloading 'em."

"You still want to be in charge?" Brad asked, not bothering to hide the mocking note in his voice.

Kara firmed her shoulders. It couldn't be that difficult. "I'll handle it."

Kara walked next to the truck, unable to help noticing how terribly large the birds suddenly seemed. Strange how much smaller and more docile they appeared when already in their pens.

"*You'll* handle it?" Brad looked far more than dubious. In fact his whole expression was a challenge.

Inspecting the large van normally used for carrying circus and zoo animals, Kara wished Brad would go away and let her figure this one out. It didn't help to have him staring at her, obviously doubting her ability.

She circled the vehicle one more time. Maybe if they just backed the van up to the corral gate...

Kara gave the directions and as the driver backed toward the gate, Brad pinned her with his gaze, allowing the extent of his skepticism to show. "You planning to open the door and let them out of the van?"

Kara, who hadn't considered that aspect, blanched, wondering what condition the birds would be in after being cooped up in the truck. What if they bolted? Swallowing her nervousness, she bluffed. "Of course I am."

Approaching the corral, she ducked in between the railing, clenching her hands as the truck backed closer, swiping suddenly sweaty palms against her cutoffs. Kara swallowed a growing lump of nervousness as she approached the back of the van. Closing her eyes for a moment and uttering a brief prayer, she unfastened the door and pulled on the rope. The door opened and she gazed upward, seeing eye to eye with one of the huge beasts. When she registered the fact that his eyeball was almost the size of a tennis ball she lost her nerve.

One black bird burst over the ramp, his hooflike claws clattering as he landed. Several brownish females followed his lead, flapping their small wings. As all the birds unloaded from the van, most of them jumping over the ramp, Kara felt a brief moment of relief. Then the van lurched forward. The driver, having seen that his charter was unloaded, drove ahead, blocking her view of the ostriches. By the time the driver stopped, the largest male bird had covered the distance to the gate and darted out of the corral.

Brad shut the gate, closing in the rest. "Okay, Kara. You've proven your oats. Now let me get the male."

Kara's stubborn streak deepened and, ignoring Brad, she ran toward the large male. The bird eyed her warily, but he didn't seem ready to attack. Aggressive by nature, the males had to be handled very carefully. Kara approached, cautiously waving her hands toward the ostrich. "Come on, birdie."

From the corner of her eye, Kara saw Brad's face fall into lines of disbelief as he mouthed the word "birdie." But from what she'd read, Kara knew the male could be eased back with the others, preferring to be in the midst of the flock. She moved closer to the bird and the ostrich started running. But to her chagrin he ran in circles. The faster she ran, the faster he ran—still in circles. Panting, she heard Brad's laughter over the clucking trills of the females in the corral.

Kara stopped running after the bird, knowing he would continue until they both dropped. It seemed despite all her reading, that the physical challenge of caring for the birds wasn't quite as elementary as the books had claimed. Kara glanced back at the corral at the females. Of course.

Before she could lose her nerve, Kara ran to the corral, picked up a long-handled stick with a loop of rope attached to the end. Kara gripped the wooden handle and edged near one of the younger females. The timid bird allowed her to loop the rope around its neck and Kara led her from the corral, careful not to let any of the others escape. When the male finally noticed the female, he stopped running and stared warily at Kara.

Cautiously she led them both back to the corral. Not certain how she'd get them both in and fasten the gate at the same time, relief whooshed through her as Brad swung the gate shut.

"Next time they try to escape, you can head them toward a round corral and wait till they drop." Amusement filled Brad's eyes, making the faint laughter lines in his face crinkle, raising Kara's hackles and her defenses.

"Very funny."

"I thought you'd read up on ostriches. They're known for running in circles."

Resentment flared again. "I'm aware of that. But reading and doing are two different things."

"My point exactly," he replied smugly, crossing his arms over his chest.

"If you don't like the way I do things, we can call off the whole deal right now!" Kara retorted.

"That might not be such a bad idea!" he replied with equal heat.

"So you've bought some new stock," a third voice chimed in.

Startled, Brad and Kara turned and stared at Erastus, who seemed to have materialized out of nowhere.

"Pure African blacks," Erastus continued as he walked toward the corral and examined the stock. "Good choice. The blacks are the least aggressive. Suited for beginners. Course blue necks grow larger, but they're more hot tempered." His wise eyes settled over them, searching their mutinous expressions.

Brad cleared his throat, trying to act as though he and Kara hadn't just been at each other's throats. "The breeder said they'd be good stock."

Erastus's gaze seemed to see too far. "Hmm. He was right." His gaze shifted to include the new stock. "Good feather quality, straight toes, no apparent scars, clear eyes. Prime stock, all right."

"But I don't think there's a mated pair in the bunch," Kara couldn't resist adding, seeing the varying ages of the birds, especially the far-too-young females.

Brad turned surprised eyes on her. "Pairs?"

Erastus chuckled. "Sure, son. No proven layers, no eggs."

"Maybe we can switch them around with some of the stock we already have," Brad suggested.

Shaking his head, Erastus continued. "Not a good idea. Hell, we had a hen who was laying and a rooster who wasn't breeding so we decided to switch the pairs' mates around. It didn't work so we switched them back. But the hen wouldn't have anything to do with the first rooster. Before we knew what had happened, she'd bounced off the fence trying to get away from him. Lost one eye and didn't survive. Nope, I wouldn't go switching them around."

Disgusted, Brad stared at the new birds. "So what do I do with them?"

"Could talk to the breeder and swap them out for pairs," Erastus suggested, as his gaze shifted between them meaningfully. "Most everything in the animal kingdom gets along better in pairs. At least that's what Sarah and me found out after we'd been married awhile."

Brad met Kara's gaze. The ranch meant too much to both of them to lose it over a juvenile fight. All they had to do was figure out the day-to-day running of an ostrich ranch. How hard could that be?

KARA SWIPED AT THE MUD on her cheek as she kept trying to clean the trough. Glancing up, she watched Brad whistling as he unloaded the feed. Her brows drew together in displeasure. It seemed he'd chosen the easier task as he'd done in several other incidents. True, he'd asked her to pick and she hadn't relished hefting hundred-pound sacks of feed. Still he didn't have to sound so blessedly *cheerful.*

Feeling an unexpected tug on her head, Kara reached out just as one of the female ostriches plucked the bandanna off her hair and escaped with it.

"Hey, stop that! You dumb bird, if you swallow that you'll croak!" Dropping her scrub brush, Kara tore off after the speeding ostrich, but by the time she reached the bird, it had already swallowed her bounty. "Fine, but don't come running to me when your stomach explodes!"

"Tsk-tsk. The point is to keep them alive, Kara. Since you know they'll peck at anything, you could keep the accessories down to a minimum."

Kara glanced at her plain jeans, T-shirt and tennis shoes. She hadn't even worn a watch, knowing how the unrepentant pickpockets carried off anything they could snatch. "I'll try to lay off the diamonds and furs," she retorted.

But Brad was looking beyond her. "Uh-oh."

She snapped around and to her dismay saw the ostriches turning over the newly cleaned trough and dragging it through the mud. "They did that on purpose!" she accused.

"Just to make your day," he countered. "Face it. The books don't tell you what quirky, neurotic beasts they really are."

"They're not neurotic," she defended.

His brows rose. "What do you call animals that get stressed out more easily than a roomful of type A personalities locked away without their cellular phones?"

"They're a little simpleminded, I'll grant you that. But if we keep things simple for them they don't get stressed out."

"Simple? Like mirrors in the nursery?"

Kara held on to her temper. Earlier she had seen a chick that had hatched alone become frantic. Searching for a way for the baby to not feel so isolated, Kara had put a mirror in the nursery pen so that it could spend the day pecking and talking to itself. It was certainly better than Brad's suggestion that they put it in with the older chicks.

"If we'd done what you'd wanted, the poor thing would have been trampled to death by the bigger birds."

"They were only a week older."

"Which is enough to put the younger ones in danger since they grow so fast. I thought—"

"Enough," he interrupted, holding up a hand to silence her. "Why don't we just deal with today's problems and not rehash yesterday's?"

She slanted a glance at him and then stalked over to the trough. He was right. It didn't help to replay their mistakes, but she couldn't believe that he didn't know *anything* about raising ostriches. She'd assumed since he was so hot to buy the ranch that he was an expert on their feathered friends. Not that he'd been thrilled to learn about her own lack of practical experience.

As she reached out to upend the unwieldy piece of metal, Brad grasped the other end of the trough and turned it over easily. She rewarded him by handing him the hose. "I'll turn on the water."

As she walked toward the spigot, Kara eyed the birds, who seemed to be intent on looking very innocent. "You're not fooling anybody," she muttered.

But they only trotted over to the other side of the pen where they tried to steal Brad's hat. Kara nearly laughed aloud, but her amusement turned into disbelief when she saw that he'd tied his hat on much as cowboys in the outback did.

Once again, he'd surprised her. But he did a lot of that.

He turned away from her and she took the opportunity to study him. Since they were forced to share close quarters, she purposely avoided looking at him. But now, in an unguarded moment she could enjoy watching the play of his muscles beneath his shirt, the way his jeans clung to well-defined thighs. Although she'd acknowledged his good looks from the first, she didn't expect them to grow more appealing each day.

He turned suddenly, catching her gaze fastened on him. Unwilling to reveal a shred of her interest, Kara feigned absorption in the feed supply at his side. However, it was difficult to look very interested in sacks of ratite pellets.

"What's so fascinating?"

Kara couldn't think of an answer so she switched subjects. "Have you checked the humidity in the incubators?"

"At least a dozen times," he replied dryly. "And the temperature, too."

"But—"

"You don't need to remind me. If either one's out of whack, we lose the chicks. We proved that already

when we lost the first batch of eggs.'' Seeing her eyebrows raise like twin war signals, he amended his
words. ''Okay, *I* lost them by not turning on the heat.
I told you these birds are a lot of trouble. Especially
since you don't know anything about raising them.''
Brad shifted the sacks of feeds, inadvertently moving
closer.

Kara licked her lips, trying to ignore his proximity.
''The return on our investment will be phenome-
nal—''

''*If* we don't kill half the stock first. Not to mention how dumb they are. Whoever heard of animals
without an instinct to live?''

''They'll have one after they're about a year old.''

''Fine, until then we pamper them.'' Brad pulled off
his hat and ran one hand through his already tousled
hair.

''And you get to own half of the best ranch in the
county,'' she said, trying not to notice how the sun
glinted on the clean sweep of his hair, the planes of his
golden skin.

''Which is the point of this whole deal,'' Brad
agreed, his ebony eyes darkening with pleasure as they
always did when the two of them spoke of owning the
ranch.

''At least for five more months,'' she added, wondering at that funny little kick her heart gave when he
smiled.

''Mother at four o'clock,'' he warned beneath his
breath, still smiling.

Kara tore her gaze from his appealing smile and realized that her mother had almost reached them.
Turning, she greeted Muriel with a wave. At the same
time, Brad draped a casual arm around her waist.

Trying not to react to his touch, Kara managed to smile at her mother.

"Hi, you two!" Muriel was practically skipping as she approached. Although always young looking, the years had fallen away since Muriel had met Chuck. Especially when he'd helped her through the first ravages of her flooded house, investing his time and labor to salvage her prized possessions. The house itself was another matter. It would have to be practically rebuilt, making Muriel a semipermanent houseguest.

Brad concentrated on not feeling the rightness of his arm around Kara, the way her body softly curved against his. She was, at best, an unwilling participant. He needed to remember that. But for now he savored the moment as Muriel captured her daughter's attention.

"Am I interrupting?" Muriel asked, glancing around at the newly washed trough, the neatly stacked piles of feed.

"Not really, Mom. We were just finishing up."

"Are you busy tonight?"

Kara glanced at Brad and saw from his expression that he would go along with Muriel's request. It was spooky the way they had come to read each other so well. Too well, Kara realized with a jolt, relishing the feel of Brad's arm as it remained around her.

"No, we're free," she replied, appalled to hear the huskiness in her voice.

"Chuck wants to know if we'd all like to go on a hayride!"

Dismay flooded Kara's face and crept into her voice. "A hayride?"

Sensitive to the abrupt change in her daughter, Muriel blinked and then managed a strained smile.

"Of course, how silly of me. A hayride's for young people. I don't know what got into me. Hanging out with you made me forget how old I really am. I'm sure Chuck will still want you both to go." She turned away.

"No!" Kara reached for her mother's hand. "That's not what I meant." She scrabbled for an excuse. "I just don't know if Brad can get away."

His smile would melt butter. "Nothing keeping me from going. Especially with the two best-looking women in the state."

Muriel smiled prettily, the cloud lifting from her face. "You're a dear man. No wonder Kara married you."

Brad rewarded her with another one of those incredible grins. "She thinks I'm pretty irresistible, too."

"I thought as much." Muriel winked at him. "And a hayride does sound like a romantic evening."

Kara kept from groaning out loud with only the greatest effort. Just what she needed—her mother and Brad cooking up intimate evenings. She couldn't back out of the hayride or her mother's feelings would be hurt. But a romantic hayride!

THE MOON CLIMBED over an ebony sky, fencing with the stars for prominence in the velvet cloak of night. Newly cut grass carpeted the field and sent its fragrance to blend with that of the creeping honeysuckle and abundant magnolia blossoms. It was a true sultry Southern evening, one ripe with promise and filled with moist fragrant breezes.

The clip-clop of horses' hooves blended with the symphony of crickets and nightingales while fireflies provided bursts of sudden light against the unending darkness. The wagon rolled mildly along, its large wheels creaking as it moved forward, swaying its inhabitants, lulling them with the gentle movement. The silvery sound of Muriel's laughter added to the night sounds.

But Brad focused only on the woman at his side. The tangy smell of her, one that tormented him nightly, now teased him anew. Kara swayed closer to him as the wagon shifted while rolling over a bump in the road.

Although he'd enjoyed goading Kara by agreeing to this hayride, it hadn't occurred to him that it would be even more difficult for him to endure this slow form of torture. Their marriage might not be real, but her body sharing the same bed every night certainly was. And it was driving him crazy. Especially since she was so stubborn and bullheaded the rest of the time.

He fully expected her wild, impulsive moves to bankrupt them in a matter of weeks. Whoever heard of giving away valuable birds because she'd heard there was a lonely orphaned baby elephant at the zoo that needed companions? The freaky thing was that the birds had indeed induced the grieving elephant to begin eating again and now they were all great buddies. Still . . .

He had to smile when he remembered how she'd dug her feet in and challenged him to deny her the privilege of helping the orphaned pachyderm. As if he'd had a chance of winning that one.

No more than he had a chance to forget her body lying next to his . . .

"Blanket?"

The nearly suggestive sounding word, considering his train of thought, jarred Brad, making him stare at

Kara's innocent-looking face. She offered a tartan stadium blanket to him and he automatically accepted the plaid wool. Luminous eyes seemed smoky green in the encroaching darkness while her golden skin gleamed beneath the moon's luster. She remained all innocence as he spread the blanket over their laps.

Then she leaned closer, the whisper of her breath near his ear. If this was a plan to have him give away the whole herd...

"I think Mother's having a good time," she whispered. "I'm still not sure what I think about Chuck, but *she* seems to like him."

"He *is* my friend," Brad said dryly. Kara certainly didn't pull any punches. She was not only willing to speak her mind; she'd take out a billboard to advertise her opinion.

"I know," she dismissed. "But your interests are hardly the same as mine. As long as Chuck flies on course, doesn't crash your plane, and shares jokes with you, he's okay. But I have a little more to consider."

"Careful. Don't want to give too much importance to my livelihood." Brad stretched out his legs.

Kara considered rewording her thoughts about Chuck, then discarded the notion. Brad only heard what he wanted to, anyway. Instead she shrugged. "It's not your only source of income."

"If you're referring to these blasted birds, I'd hardly call our venture a rousing success yet."

"That's because you're so stuffy." She kept her voice from rising with an effort, determined not to ruin her mother's outing.

"You mean because I want to run cost projections?"

"A ranch is land and feeling and people, not squiggles in that mountain of books you keep."

"You better be glad I have more than a molehill of business sense since you seem hell-bent on bankrupting us."

"Four birds, Brad. Not the whole flock. And any compassionate human being could see—"

"That you're an easy touch. I'm partners with a woman who'd sooner give away the profits than build a future." And a woman who now challenged him with the fire in her glance, the lilt of her body. Losing the thread of the argument, he shifted away from her, hearing the gentle murmurs of the other couple. In another time and another place he'd have pursued Kara, but she'd made it abundantly clear that her only interest in him was the ranch.

Just then she leaned close to him. "Mother's watching."

Obligingly he draped an arm around her. It was a delicious sort of torment. One he was beginning to indulge in too often. Her face was close to his, the dewy softness of her skin beckoning to him. From this proximity he could see the sprinkle of freckles that danced across the bridge of her nose, the moist fullness of her lips in the moonlight. Ignoring the logic that told him not to, he reached toward those inviting lips.

Her "oh" of surprise allowed him to slide his tongue inside to explore and incite. At first, she seemed frozen by shock, then slowly, insidiously, she responded. Like a mating ritual, their mouths danced with touches and invisible caresses and soon the air between them grew hot with need and desire.

Surprise gripped Kara even as she felt the slide of Brad's lips against hers, the strength in his arms as he held her. His face bent toward hers and she felt the spiral of shocked yearning arrow through her, weakening her body, dissolving her defenses. Liquid heat pooled, then coursed through each sharpened nerve ending. One hand cupped the back of her neck, moving with a swirling motion that made her want to moan her satisfaction. He used the pad of his thumb on the other hand to skim her cheek, then slide slowly down the length of her neck.

Hearing a faint set of chuckles, Kara suddenly remembered this was supposed to be for show and they in fact had an audience. Breaking away from Brad, Kara deliberately held her body stiff within his embrace. A glance at her mother brought a rewarding smile. Apparently they were fooling Muriel rather well. And if working with a formidable opponent like Brad was more difficult than she bargained for, the reward of seeing her mother happy was worth it. It was this other part of their charade that was more disturbing to her. Earth-shattering kisses that were mere pretense to him left her feeling like a fallout victim. A foolish victim who craved more.

Funny, it didn't seem to bother Brad that they were thrown into such close proximity. Of course, he was probably used to beautiful women throwing themselves at him. What was one more female, even if she was the one sharing his bed?

Glancing around, she saw Chuck staring at them, his eyes filling with speculation. Great, all she needed. The court jester. If her mother hadn't deserved a fair shake at happiness, Kara would have had words for the pilot who seemed intent on making them squirm. Instead she nestled closer into Brad's embrace, trying to convince Chuck that she'd enjoyed their showy kiss.

Startled, Brad stared down at her as she tipped her face upward and purred, "Isn't this supposed to be romantic?"

Sensing her heat beside him, he felt an answering response and was fairly certain she hadn't been simply acting. The curve of her breasts teased his chest and he was suddenly glad for the weight of the blanket draped over him.

MURIEL SHIFTED for the fourth time in as many minutes.

"Uncomfortable?" Chuck asked.

"I'd just like to stretch my legs a bit." She glanced ruefully at the cramped space.

"I can make some room," he offered.

"In a wagon?"

He grinned. "Leave it to me." He raised his voice, booming into the quiet. "What do you mean you dropped it?"

Kara and Brad snapped their heads back to stare at him.

Chuck looked distraught as he stared over the side of the wagon. "Muriel's dropped her bracelet. Can you two move farther to the edge and look?"

Since they were sitting near the back of the wagon, Kara and Brad obligingly scooted forward, dropping their legs over the open tailgate.

In a swift movement, Chuck leaned forward and pushed each of them square in the back. At the same time he shouted to the driver. "Go faster, step on it!"

The wagon lurched forward, picking up speed as Kara and Brad tumbled into the shallow grassy slope of the ditch bank.

"But we need to stop and get them!" Muriel protested.

Chuck smiled. "No, I'm *sure* they want to be alone."

"But—"

"We can send the wagon back to get them." He settled closer to Muriel, draping one arm around her and pulling her next to him. "In good time, of course."

"I'm not sure—"

"You talk too much, Muriel. Especially for a beautiful woman."

KARA FELT THE AIR whoosh from her lungs as she and Brad landed in a tangled mess of arms and legs. But the foremost sensation was the uncompromising length of him pressed against her. When it was clear they had stopped rolling, she looked at him cautiously. It was difficult, despite the play of moonlight, to see what he was thinking. True, his breath seemed labored, but they'd just fallen out of a wagon. *Been pushed,* she corrected herself, but even that thought faded as Brad continued to stare at her.

His chest trapped her breasts, his belt buckle indented her skin, they were so close. His legs lay heavily on hers. And his gaze never left her eyes.

She pushed the words out. "Shouldn't...we see about the wagon?"

"Wagon?"

Numbly she nodded her head, wondering if he would dip his head and kiss her. It seemed by the angle of his head that he could....

Her thoughts blurred as his mouth descended on hers, not gently seeking this time. Instead it was an assured movement, one that spoke of possessiveness. She wondered briefly about that, then surrendered to the sensations he evoked. Overwhelmed by his clean male scent, the hard length of his body, she responded by reaching for his chest, then curling her hands around his neck, finally twining her fingers in the provocative length of dark hair.

Brad countered by running his hands lightly down the length of her body, teasing, tormenting as she moved restlessly beneath him. Not certain if she wanted to escape or beg for more, she sucked in her breath when one hand paused near her breast, gently kneading the tingling flesh through the thin material of her shirt. When his hands grasped her buttons and easily unfastened them, she felt first the rush of warm air, then the flicker of his mouth as it savored her skin. In a moment, she knew her bra might easily be dispatched along with the remainder of her willpower.

Gathering the last of her sanity, she spoke, hearing the seeds of passion in her husky, deepened tones. "Shouldn't we go catch the wagon?"

For a moment he stiffened and she waited to hear the expected protest. To hear that he'd rather stay with her, to ignore the pretense, to give up the charade. Instead, he rolled away. "Right, we'd better get going."

He held out a hand and helped her up. Purposely she ignored the stab of disappointment she felt, knowing it was ridiculous to feel let down that he hadn't argued against her logic. "Thanks."

Together they climbed the shallow incline. But neither spoke. Amazement prevented it. The wagon was disappearing around the bend, illuminated only by the fragile moonlight. Even if they were sprint runners they couldn't catch up with the now fast moving vehicle since it had gained a considerable head start. Which left them alone in the dark Texas night, the imprints of each other's bodies still as fresh as the grass clinging to their clothes.

Chapter Six

Kara pounded in the fence posts, giving them far more whacks than necessary. Imagining Chuck's head perched on one of the posts provided added vigor. Between him and her mother, his obviously willing accomplice, they were providing far too many antics for comfort. Just thinking of the previous evening spewed out a mixture of frustration and, worse, longing.

"Those need to be set in cement."

Kara whirled around to see Brad lounging against one of the first posts she'd put in. "Says who?"

"They won't be sturdy enough." He frowned. "And they need to be closer together."

"Since when are you an expert on building ostrich pens?"

He shrugged. "Admittedly I don't like to run a business on the fly-by-the-seat-of-my-pants method. But I've found research to be helpful."

She snorted. "Said like a true greenhorn."

He lifted his brows. "Unlike an expert versed on ranching via the public library?"

Fuming, she ignored the appealing silhouette of his body, the stance of his long legs as he stood and watched her. How had she ever imagined that she could live with this man for six months and remain unaffected? And despite her anxiety, the days were ticking away with disturbing speed.

A sudden memory of his body crushing hers flashed into her mind. Not that she hadn't spent the night reliving the moment, along with the solitary evening they'd spent together walking back to the barn after Muriel and Chuck had disappeared. After the initial shock of being ditched had subsided, they'd enjoyed the forced intimacy.

Her mouth lifted in a smile as she recalled how Brad had entertained her on the walk home. Laughing, teasing, then finally serenading her in the moonlight with silly songs that convulsed them both, he had made it seem like a magical time. One she hadn't wanted to end. When they'd climbed into the bed, she'd almost hoped they could continue where the kiss had stopped. Then remembering it was a business arrangement, she'd purposely turned her back on Brad and that notion. But part of her still wondered....

She shook her head. Just because they enjoyed each other's company and he made her laugh as no one ever had didn't mean that he felt the same way about her. Despite the passion in their kisses ...

She was surprised at how much fun Brad was when he loosened up. Almost like a different person. Like a man she would have wanted to notice her in any other situation. In fact, the more she knew of him, the more she liked. She wondered if he felt a fraction of what she did. If he, too, wondered what they could be sharing if they hadn't signed a contract that forced them into unnatural roles.

Brad bent down to examine the wire she'd purchased to build the pens. His jeans stretched tight and Kara felt her mouth go dry. At the same time, he twisted around with a disapproving glare. "This wire isn't heavy enough."

Great. Gawk at him like an idiot. This was supposed to be a business deal. Nothing else. You may be making cow's eyes at him, but he hasn't forgotten why we're together.

Defensively she glanced at the wire she'd purchased. It wasn't as heavy a gauge as one that had been in the diagram in her book, but it was considerably cheaper.

"This wire will be fine. It's not like we're trying to fence in elephants." She squatted down beside him, reaching out to test the wire. Brad lifted his hands at the same time, grazing hers. Kara drew in a deep breath, trying not to tremble as his flesh warmed hers. Jerkily she sat back, trying to control her shallow breathing.

Except for a small tick in his jaw, Brad looked unaffected. "Those birds kick like mules, not to mention how they peck everything to pieces."

"I thought you wanted to save money," she chided. "Aren't you the one who said *I* was trying to bankrupt the ranch?"

He threw up his hands. "Fine, but when this thing falls apart, remember it was all your idea."

"I'm no welsher."

"You saying I am?" He pushed his hat back, daring her to reply.

She had to get away from this forced closeness. "Didn't you say we needed to collect eggs?"

The look on his face told her he hadn't missed her not too subtle change of subject. "Right. But this time try not to get us killed, okay?"

Refusing to answer, she wished she could tell him he was full of baloney. But unfortunately he was right. All of her book learning hadn't prepared her for the dominant males that sat on the nests, aggressively protecting the eggs. And their first attempt at collecting eggs had been a disaster.

As they approached the nesting area, she and Brad glanced at each other apprehensively. Right now it would have been nice if one of them *had* been an expert, because reading only took her so far.

Brad seemed to be in tune with her thoughts. "The male was skittish last time we locked him in the shed. He looked pretty stressed."

Kara's eyes met Brad's and then slid away. If they stressed out the male it could put him off breeding. But it wasn't a subject Kara wanted to touch. It hit too close to home.

Instead she gazed into the pen, meeting the regal gaze of the male. In the wild, to protect the eggs, the males often stretched their necks forward on the ground as they sat on the nest, resembling a large ungainly hump on the grassy plains. Their behavior had led to the mistaken belief that ostriches buried their heads in the sand. They did no such thing, but old fables died hard.

"Instead of locking him in the shed this time, why don't I distract him and then you can dive in and get the eggs," Brad suggested.

Kara tried to keep her grin under control. "Why don't I distract him? He seems to have taken a nasty disliking to you."

Brad wanted to argue that it was more dangerous to be the person doing the distracting, but Kara was probably right. She'd developed a natural affinity for the birds, while the ostriches had cultivated a growing dislike for him. "Okay, but don't take any chances."

Kara's saucy smile hit him somewhere in the gut. "Now, now. Don't go all mushy on me."

Brad watched as she tossed her hair back, its gold glinting in the sunlight. His gaze followed her tall, slender form as she approached the pen. Lured by her in the most unexpected circumstances, Brad wished, not for the first time, that they weren't locked into a business agreement that she clearly wanted to remain impersonal. Because he'd gone way beyond impersonal.

Seeing that Kara had successfully baited the male into approaching to investigate the shiny bits of color she held in both hands, Brad darted in, scooped up the eggs and exited as quickly.

But as he glanced up, Brad saw the male heading back toward Kara, murder clear in his eyes. Breaking into a run, Brad grabbed for Kara, ignoring her startled protest as he half dragged her into the shed, slamming the door shut on the incoming bird.

A hoof hit the door with a loud clang and Brad grimaced, imagining that same blow landing on Kara, crushing her fragile body.

"Why'd you do that?" she was demanding with annoyance. "What about the eggs? Don't you know they're worth—"

"More than your life?" he countered dangerously, pushing his face close to hers, his eyes glittering. "Would it be worth it to have the male crush you to

bits instead of taking out his hostility on the shed
door? Is that what you want?"

"But—"

Brad didn't let her finish, instead jerking her toward him, crushing her lips beneath his.

Her faint noises of protest were lost, muffled against
the firm flesh of his lips, the desire that surged forward as he fitted their bodies together. She felt her
breasts crush into the unyielding expanse of his chest,
her hips sliding into the cradle of his legs, her wom-
anhood pulsing against his straining arousal.

His strong fingers held her head mercilessly in a grip
that seemed meant to punish, yet only sent off a string
of signals that warned her that frustrated passion had
built to a bursting point.

They broke apart, panting. Brad's already inscru-
table eyes darkened and Kara suspected an explosion
of sorts was building.

The bird kicked at the door again, harder this time.
But the noise barely distracted Brad. "We're stuck in
here, you know." His voice was matter-of-fact, but the
expression in his face wasn't.

She sensed a challenge, one she wanted to run from.
Yet at the same time, she wanted to demand to know
if he felt anything more than a passing desire. To ask
why his grip had been so angry, so possessive. Instead
she glanced at the blank walls of the shed, purposely
keeping her voice light. "And me without my mink
and pearls."

His eyes traveled slowly over the thin cotton of her
T-shirt and the tight-fitting jeans she wore. "So it
seems."

Unable to read the meaning behind those simple
words, she stepped away from him, nervously clasp-

ing her arms in front of her chest. "How long do you think he'll stay out there?"

"Till someone distracts him," Brad replied shortly, glancing around the small, confining space.

Kara's hopes sank. He was right, of course. And that meant waiting until Chuck or her mother noticed they were missing. As she watched, Brad smoothed out a square on the floor.

"Pull up some hay, Kara. Your legs will give out standing there."

She sighed. They were stuck, and avoiding him wouldn't change that. Still she didn't want to sit so close to him in the already shrinking space. But he didn't comment further, instead stretching out his long legs, preparing to wait. Feeling foolish, she dropped down beside him.

Silence stained the air for several moments, and Kara felt driven to dispel it. "I never did like small, cooped-up places."

"Me, either."

Another long silence ensued and Kara stirred restlessly. "You never told me how you got into the air charter business."

Brad closed his eyes briefly and Kara wondered if she was irritating him, or worse, boring him. Then he turned his gaze on her. "It's not something I talk about much. My brother left me the first plane. It meant the world to him and I had to make that count for something."

Suddenly sobered, she stared at him. "You lost your brother?"

He nodded and she sensed the pain in that silence. "I think he'd be proud of you."

Surprise flickered across his face. "Todd taught me to fly. I was just a green kid with more of a penchant for trouble than anything else. But he made me reach for the stars."

"I'm sorry he's not here to share all this with you," she replied softly, struck by the pain she saw in Brad's eyes.

"Me, too. But he couldn't stick around any longer."

The import of his words struck her and she glanced up sharply. Meeting Brad's gaze, she knew she guessed correctly. "I'm really sorry."

"He wasn't a coward," Brad asserted. His tone was fierce, defensive, protective.

Kara reached out to touch his arm. "We all have our private demons."

"His had a convenient label. Postwar trauma. Todd didn't die when he was shot down and captured in the war. But he died a little at a time after that, until he just couldn't stand it any more."

Kara struggled against the knot in her throat, knowing the pain of loss. Slipping one arm to crook beneath his, she leaned against him in a comforting gesture. "So Holbrook Enterprises is a family business then."

Her understanding stunned him. Most people thought his concept was either foolish or sentimental. No one had taken it at face value when he told them the business belonged to both him and to Todd. "You could say that."

"Family's important to me. Always has been."

Brad couldn't keep the wry note from his voice. "Could have fooled me."

She punched him lightly. "Okay, so I went a little overboard with my mother. She's had enough pain in her life without knowing I'd repeated her mistake."

"Which was?"

Kara bent her head, looking as though she debated her answer. "My parents' marriage wasn't a happy one." She glanced up quickly, a pained expression in her eyes. "My father really loved her, but he was so much older that I think he swept her off her feet. And when reality set in, she realized that she was married to a far older man, with few interests in common...and that she didn't really love him." Kara twisted her fingers and forced the words out haltingly. "She respected him and was very fond of him, but all that time she longed for her grand passion, the love that would sweep all other concerns out the door. But she couldn't leave my father because she knew it would devastate him. Then he died unexpectedly when I was a teenager and the guilt nearly killed her. She thought she should have given him more."

"Maybe it was enough for him," Brad suggested.

Kara shrugged, her throat clogged with the memories, reliving those terrible times. "She never realized how happy she made him. Even though he knew."

Brad's voice was quiet. "Are you sure about that?"

Kara met his gaze directly without flinching. "You know when someone loves you, or if they're pretending because they have to."

Brad didn't seem to have an answer. Instead he reached out to hold her hand, his grasp comforting as the wave of memories crashed about them both, reminding them of their own loveless match.

KARA PENCILED IN the pair's identification on the egg's sturdy shell so she could be sure of its parentage when it hatched. It was something she'd learned to do in a costly manner. The first eggs she'd collected hadn't been identified and they weren't salable. With the price paid for eggs and chicks, the record-keeping system had to be meticulously maintained. It was something that Kara had balked at, but Brad remained firm. She might want to fly by the seat of her pants, but their customers wanted to know what they were getting.

She and Brad finished identifying the eggs that hadn't broken in their mad dash to the shed. Fortunately Chuck had stopped by to speak with Brad and had rescued them after only a few hours in the shed. But Kara hadn't minded the time. Oddly she still felt the healing process that had bound them together in those hours. She'd never revealed such personal things about herself to another human being. But the forced closeness and Brad's own revelations had conspired to make it seem natural.

Together they walked along, both deliberately keeping to opposite sides of the path. As they passed some clover in the grass, Kara paused to pick several leaves.

Brad glanced down at his clipboard. "Don't forget to mark the cards. The last time—"

"I know, I know. Are you always so persnickety?"

"It's a good thing one of us is. Unless you want to run the ranch into bankruptcy before we even get started."

Kara looked away and saw Muriel approaching. Launching up on her toes, Kara kissed him lightly instead of replying. Surprise filled his eyes, before another smoldering emotion took over. Instead of releasing her, he pulled her closer, deepening the kiss.

Kara considered pulling back, but the effect of being held by him, kissed by him, numbed her brain as effectively as an anesthetic. Remembering the evidence of his arousal when they were in the shed, she leaned against him, feeling his hipbones abrade hers, his chest tantalize the crush of her breasts.

"I hate to interrupt..." Muriel began tentatively, holding up a tray containing a pitcher of lemonade and three glasses.

Brad pulled back reluctantly, disappointment replacing the passion in his eyes as he realized he'd just put on a show for his mother-in-law. But, as quickly, he hid that sinking feeling, instead smiling heartily.

"You're never an interruption," he replied smoothly. "Kara and I were just sealing an agreement."

"Oh?" Muriel tried to look noncommittal rather than curious.

"And I have some work to do," Brad continued. "If you'll excuse me, I'll take a rain check on that lemonade."

"If you're sure I'm not running you off—"

"No." Brad's gaze centered on Kara. "You're not."

As he walked away, both women stared after him. Kara couldn't avoid releasing a regretful sigh.

"I *did* interrupt!" Muriel exclaimed. "I knew it. I should have—"

"It's fine, Mom." Kara picked up the basket of eggs and moved it off the bench, clearing a place for them to sit. "Brad and I have... all the time in the world."

"I'm so glad you met him," Muriel mused. "So different from your other boyfriends. I never felt that you let yourself get too close to them. I was beginning to wonder if you'd ever fall in love...or know true happiness.''

Kara felt the emotions choking her throat, closing off any reassuring words.

"But when I see you and Brad together,'' Muriel continued, her voice and expression equally soft, "I know you've found true love. I couldn't bear to think of you in a relationship that was anything else.'' Her mind drifted toward the past to her own loveless marriage. Then she turned her smile to include their surroundings. "And now you have this beautiful home...at least it will be again when the repairs are finished...and it's one that will finally provide a job with the freedom you need.''

Kara laughed to dislodge the sob that threatened. "You know me too well.''

"You weren't meant for offices and briefcases. I knew that the first time I set you in your sandbox and found you two minutes later digging in the mud near the ditch bank. No confinements or neat packages for you.''

"Trying to say I'm a slob?''

Muriel skirted her glance over Kara's casual clothes. "Nope. On you a T-shirt and jeans is a knockout combination. And it's clear that Brad agrees.''

Kara tried to ignore the painful hitch that comment caused. It also made her determined never to let her mother know what a farce this marriage really was. It was bad enough they were fooling a nice man like Erastus Jones. It would be another altogether to hurt her mother. Kara tried to dismiss the compliment. "You're just prejudiced.''

"Possibly. But I'm right." She glanced around at the baskets of eggs yet to be recorded. "If I helped you with this, could we be finished soon?"

"Sure. Why?"

"Thought maybe we could do a little shopping."

"I told you to borrow anything you want, Mom."

Muriel hedged. "I want something kind of special."

"Nothing I have will do? Maybe I should be insulted." Tossing back her hair, Kara laughed as she teased. "What's up? You have a date?"

"Well, sort of." Muriel studied the toe of her shoes as though they were highly fascinating.

Kara felt a twinge of alarm. Although her mother liked Chuck, Kara wasn't so sure of the irreverent pilot. He seemed ninety percent baloney. She didn't know about the remaining ten percent, but the statistics weren't encouraging. She hadn't liked that they'd gone on the hayride together, but that had seemed more like a group activity than an actual date. Still she cleared her throat and tried to sound nonjudgmental. "Where are you going for this *date?*"

Apparently she didn't succeed. Muriel straightened up. "The third degree?"

"Of course not," Kara replied indignantly. "Just healthy interest. But if you don't want to tell me . . ."

"Don't go all dramatic on me. It's not like we're running off to Vegas to elope."

Kara choked on the lemonade she'd sipped and started coughing. Jumping up, Muriel patted her on the back. "Lift your left arm, dear. Just like when you were young. You always did have a propensity to choke on the least little thing."

Gasping, Kara obeyed, hoping she could get through the shopping expedition. And the remainder of her allotted time with Brad.

RESTLESS, KARA STALKED through the ranch house. Part of her discontent was tied into worry over her mother, who'd departed for her date with Chuck. She didn't want Chuck to reveal the truth about her marriage to Brad. But the majority of her restlessness was tied to something she couldn't quite put her finger on. One she suspected had far too much to do with Brad.

Walking to the window of the living room, Kara stared into the darkness, relieved only by the still, bright moon. She trailed her fingers along the back of the couch and stared at Brad's recliner with distaste. He hadn't budged about the ugly piece of furniture. She had suggested they move it into the study, but he'd refused, saying that Erastus had fixed up the study just right and he didn't want to change a thing. Since he'd used the same excuse about the den, she suspected his true motive was in needling her, because she disliked the chair so much.

Her gaze shifted from the chair to rest on the table beside it. She hadn't grown to like his grisly collection of items any better, either.

Lifting her head, Kara heard Brad's footsteps. They headed down the hall, through the kitchen. In another moment, the kitchen door opened and closed. Narrowing her eyes, Kara stared at the offensive chair. *No time like the present.*

With a great deal of huffing and puffing, she dragged the chair through the doorway and down the hall to the den. Since it was one room that was sparsely furnished, there was plenty of room for the chair. Of course, there was plenty of room in the living room, as well, she acknowledged, as she lugged the cumbersome recliner into the room.

Fortunately the doorways were wide and tall, allowing her to move the chair through easily. After she positioned it in the most inconspicuous spot, she returned to the living room and viewed the area with satisfaction. Much better. Now her grandmother's Victorian sofa didn't look as though it had been housed in a garage sale. And Aunt Tillie definitely looked happier. Kara glanced at the table. At least she would if that fertility goddess would disappear.

But one thing at a time.

Wondering where Brad had gone, Kara decided to go upstairs and take a warm bath. Inhaling the woodsy scent of Brad's soap and shampoo, she allowed herself to imagine him standing in the shower with the water sluicing over his well-formed body. She reached out to touch his washcloth and towel, still damp from his shower. It was as though everything about him permeated the room, from his razor and shaving lotion to the cologne she often uncapped to sneak a whiff. It was a torturous luxury, sharing the same bathroom with him. Their towels rested side by side, as though they belonged together. It was oddly intimate, strangely beguiling.

Deciding to indulge, Kara lit candles and added a handful of her best bath salts before climbing into a steaming tub. It was easy to imagine Brad relaxing in the same tub, his long legs stretched out to fill the plentiful space. A smile played about her lips at the thought. Staying in until she was prunelike, Kara felt herself drifting until she heard masculine whistling. Bolting upright, she pulled the plug in the tub and stepped out. After quickly toweling off, she donned her oversize terry robe and scuffs.

A quick glance in the mirror showed curling tendrils at her temples and forehead. The rest of her hair remained in a loose topknot. Deciding to forgo any other examination, Kara raced from the room, knowing she had to see the effect of her furniture arranging on Brad.

Trying to be inconspicuous, she sidled past the opening to the study where the television was playing. She darted into the living room and paused. The chair was still gone. Her hopes brightened. Maybe he wasn't a total Neanderthal. Raising her glance to exchange a triumphant look with Aunt Tillie, Kara's mouth opened in shock. The painting was gone!

First she searched the den. Tillie wasn't there. Racing down the hall, she skidded to a halt at the doorway to the study. Trying to look nonchalant, she entered, nervously retying her robe.

Brad glanced up, with a knowing smile. "Want to watch the game?"

"No! That is...maybe for a while." Not willing to bring up the subject of missing items, even though she knew *he* had to be the one to have taken the painting, Kara eased into a chair.

She stared unseeing at the television while the silence between them mounted.

"Popcorn?" Brad's voice broke the quiet, shattering her prickly nerves.

"No." She waved her hand away from the bowl he offered. "Not right now."

"I'm pretty full, too. I went and picked up a pizza."

She feigned innocence. "Really?"

"Yep. Delivery boy was sick. One of the pitfalls of living in the country."

"Right." The pendulum clock on the mantel ticked in harmony with the sportscaster's voice. Where could he have put the painting? Surely he hadn't done anything drastic with it.

But from the smug look on his face, she wondered.

"Okay, what did you do with it?"

He glanced up innocently. "With what?"

"You know what. Aunt Tillie."

"I'll make you a deal. I'll leave my chair in the nether regions of the house if you'll agree to pack Aunt Tillie into the attic."

She shook her head. "No way."

"Then my chair goes back in the living room."

Kara got to her feet, gritting her teeth. "I want to know what you've done with my aunt."

"Still protecting her virtue after all these years? No wonder she looks so dried up."

Kara advanced on him.

He gestured across the hallway. "She's in the dining room, scaring the varnish off the china cabinet."

Tossing her head, Kara left for the dining room. Aunt Tillie was perched in an unladylike sprawl, upside down on top of the cabinet. After retrieving the painting, Kara dusted off the hand-carved frame. She doubted her prim aunt had experienced this much excitement in her lifetime. A kidnapping and rescue all in one evening.

Hearing the distinctive sound of the recliner being moved back into the living room, she repressed a groan. She wondered if he would believe that the chair could spontaneously combust. She'd certainly enjoy torching the ugly thing.

But even as she completed the thought, Brad poked his head around the door. "I'll turn off the game if you want to watch something else."

She started to shake her head, then realized he was offering an olive branch. "Sure. I love musical comedy."

Seeing his face fall, she grinned, enjoying herself. "Or a long, meaty foreign film with subtitles. Good thing we have a VCR."

With effort he kept his expression relatively even. "I'll go stock up on some reinforcements...that is refreshments. You want some of that pizza now?"

"One piece," she agreed. Dinner had been a rushed affair, what with the shopping trip and then getting Muriel ready for her date.

While Brad headed for the kitchen, Kara rehung the portrait in the living room and then started searching through her collection of videotapes in the study. Picking one out, she put it in the machine.

When Brad returned, looking both martyred and resigned, she waited until he'd settled on the couch beside her before pressing the play button on the remote control.

His face registered complete surprise when *The Hunt for Red October* flashed on the screen.

"It *is* set in a foreign country," she offered.

"Subtitles?" he asked, his lips twitching.

"I guess I got those mixed up with the credits. Sorry."

"I'm not."

"Don't tell me you were being *nice* by agreeing to watch my kind of movie," she teased.

His eyes met hers. "It's not often I'm that nice."

She wondered if it was a warning.

Within a short time, popcorn was scattered between them. The entire box of pizza had been retrieved from the kitchen, polished off, and its box left on the coffee table as evidence of their feast.

Nervously Kara got up to pace before a third of the movie had aired.

"This the way you usually watch a movie?" Brad asked.

"What if Chuck spills the beans?" she demanded, pivoting to stare at him.

"I knew this wasn't going to be a relaxing evening," he muttered.

"I mean it. They could get to talking, one thing leads to another—"

"Like why we got married?" he asked in disbelief.

"Do you know where they were going?"

Brad stared at her. "The Brown Palace. Why?"

But the wheels were already clicking. "We could just drop by, tell them we came in for a drink...no, they wouldn't buy that. We could tell them we wanted to make it a foursome. That's it. A foursome!" She gazed at him expectantly. "What do you think?"

"That you're nuts."

"Thanks."

Brad frowned. "But I'm with you. I wish Chuck would back off."

"I know why I do. But what's your reason?"

"Because it's hard enough to pull off this fake marriage thing with just your mother to contend with. But having Chuck over here, egging things on..."

Kara agreed completely. Chuck was like a mischievous little imp, stirring their already sticky mess into an unwieldy glob.

"But what can we do?"

Brad met her eyes. "I'll think of something."

Kara hesitated. "I don't want to hurt my mother. But I think she'll be hurt less if it ends before she gets any more involved."

"Spoken like a devoted daughter."

"You just said—"

"I know what I said. But you need to remember that your mother's not ready to be put out to pasture just yet." Anticipating Kara's interruption, he held up his hand and cut her off at the pass. "I'll do what I can to break this up, but be prepared in the future. She's liable to meet someone else."

Kara drew out her words slowly. "She never has before."

"You mean she hasn't dated anyone since your father died?"

"No. I never thought she wanted to."

Brad tucked away that bit of information. Maybe it would help discourage Chuck. "Any chance I'm going to get out of this?"

"Nope," she replied cheerfully. "I'll be dressed in a minute."

His eyes met hers. "If you have to."

Breath quickening, she fought to sound unaffected, knowing it was a lie. "I'll make the trip worth your while."

He stepped closer, his hand reaching out to skim her cheek. "I'll hold you to that."

NERVOUSLY KARA STEPPED onto the dance floor of the Brown Palace, wondering why she'd made such an idiotic promise to Brad. If she hadn't insisted on coming here, they could be at home comfortably watching videos. Instead every nerve jangled as she searched for her mother and tried to quash the prickling sensation she felt from Brad's loose hold around her waist. She remembered those fingers moving over her pliant flesh and was glad of the darkness hiding her flush.

The sensuous notes of a slow dance wound through the dim lighting and pleasure registered on Brad's face as he guided her onto the dance floor. Background sounds faded, replaced only by the gentle swish of skirts as the women dipped to the music and the soft thump of western boots moving across the wooden planks. Close to Brad, Kara breathed in his pleasing smell, recognizing the thrill she felt being held in his arms. Moist breath trilled by her ear and an answering heat formed somewhere in her core.

Feeling safe on the crowded dance floor, Kara discarded a few inhibitions, allowing her body to meld into his. Pressed against his chest, her nipples hardened, and a thrilling dampness signaled a continuing desire.

What was it about this man that made her want to forget her lifetime goals in favor of reckless passion? Business, she reminded herself. Desire, her heart argued back. Ignoring the warring inner voices, Kara swayed to the music, delighting in the command Brad showed in leading them in the dance steps. As in every other aspect, he was in control here. And something about that secretly appealed to her.

A slow two-step began. Brad's long legs were pressed against hers as they nudged her into the intricate steps of the dance. In typical fashion, one of her hands was looped about his neck, the other rested near his back, gripping his belt. It was a curiously intimate dance, one in which she had to remain close to know which step to take next. As they swayed and shifted to the song, she could feel the temperature of her blood soar.

When the dance ended, she wanted to protest. A fast rendition of the "Cotton Eye Joe" began and she moved with Brad as he led them from the dance floor and over to the bar. But he headed away from the unoccupied stools in the center of the bar, instead seating them behind a scraggly potted palm. After ordering their drinks, he turned and gently pointed her back toward the dance floor. Her stool swiveled, then stopped as she looked among the dancers. Remembering their reason for coming here, she tried to pick out her mother. But Brad was urgently nudging her. Suddenly she heard her mother's voice and bent to peek through the branches of the palm.

MURIEL WHIRLED to the last notes of the "Cotton Eye Joe" and then turned, flushed and laughing to Chuck. "We've danced every single dance!"

"Tired?"

"Not at all," she admitted. "I even loved the line dancing."

An old-fashioned waltz began, changing the mood of the fast-paced dance hall. Chuck held out his hands and Muriel stepped into them.

His strong arms circled her and she felt petite and protected within his hold. He was nearly a foot taller, making her tip her head back to see the expression in his light blue eyes. Although normally she saw laughter there, it was something else she saw now.

He guided them to the tune of the song and she wondered briefly just how long it had been since she'd been in a man's embrace. It was easy to calculate. Far too long.

Chuck bent his head down and his breath trailed across her neck. A shiver of anticipation and delight chased through her. It was difficult to readjust her thinking. She'd put the possibility of romance out of her life for so long that she felt awkward, unsure of herself.

But Chuck wasn't treating her as though she were past her prime, a woman consigned to the over-the-hill group. Instead he ignited long-buried feelings. Along with dormant, nearly extinct passion. By treating her as though she were something special, he was beginning to make her feel just that way.

Another couple bumped into them and Chuck tightened his hold on her. Muriel sucked in her breath as their bodies melded as close together as possible.

His breathing seemed suddenly shallower and Muriel could feel the heat that flowed between them. The music was ending and Chuck drew her off the dance floor.

They moved toward the bar and she thought she saw Kara and Brad disappearing behind a tattered-looking potted plant. "I must be going crazy. I could swear that was Kara and Brad."

"You're completely sane and it is."

"What in the world?" Muriel glanced at him in confusion.

"I think it's called spying," he replied dryly.

"Whatever for?"

"Apparently they don't trust the old folks when they're not at home," Chuck replied, before ordering their drinks. "How about giving them a run for their money?"

Muriel laughed. "I'm game."

BRAD SAW THEM COMING and quickly swept Kara onto the dance floor. But it seemed that Chuck and Muriel were on a direct path toward them. Dancing so fast they were attracting attention, Kara and Brad zoomed across the floor, barely missing several collisions.

"Do you think they spotted us?" Kara asked worriedly. "I don't want them to think that we're... well..."

"Doing what we're doing?" Brad guided them past the main cluster of dancers but out of the corner of his eye he saw Chuck gaining on them. "Hell." They were approaching a door marked Storage. "Hang on." Holding her with one arm, Brad reached for the door with the other, swung them inside and shut it quickly.

Not hearing anything for a few seconds, he released a gusty breath. "I think we're safe." At that moment a distinctive click echoed in the small, dark room.

"I hope that's not what it sounded like," Kara offered in a reedy voice.

Brad rattled the knob, suspecting before he did that it wouldn't move. "Well, Mata Hari. Looks like Chuck nailed us. And I don't imagine anyone will hear us until the band quits playing."

Kara sank against the wall with a groan. "You think he'll tell her everything now?"

"I think we've got more important things to worry about. Like getting out of here."

Kara arched an uncharacteristically provocative look at him. "Oh, I don't know. I'm getting kind of used to being stuck with you."

Chapter Seven

"A hot tub?" Brad circled the new delivery and stared first at Kara and then at Erastus.

"It was ordered a long time ago and goes with the ranch as one of the fixtures," Erastus explained as he shifted his hat back. "Yep, couldn't get the money back now if I wanted to. Might as well go ahead and let the men install it."

"But it hardly seems fair," Kara protested. "It wasn't part of the purchase price."

"Oh yes, it was, little lady. Look in the contract. It's listed under fixtures."

"Funny, I never noticed that," Brad said, frowning.

"And if anyone would notice every dotted *I* and crossed *T*..." Kara added.

"See you two still have that spark," Erastus commented as the workers unloaded the hot tub along with a pile of redwood for the accompanying deck to install it on.

"Spark...well, yes," Brad answered, shooting Kara a look. While they might point out each other's liabilities when alone, it wasn't a wise idea to do it in front of Erastus.

"I like to tease," Kara offered lamely, a warmth settling in her midsection as she thought of the previous evening. Being locked in the storeroom until after two in the morning had been a most interesting diversion. One she'd hugged warmly to her chest the rest of the night even while trying to remain unaffected lying in the same bed with Brad.

"Keeps things lively," Erastus agreed. "Dull just gets duller. But when two people have that special spark, things just get better and better."

Weakly Kara smiled back, guilt nudging her as they continued to bamboozle this delightful old man. "You and Sarah must have been very happy."

"Success is satisfying for a while," Erastus replied. "And so is wealth. But nothing takes the place of love. Me and Sarah had a lot of mighty good years together. And I wouldn't trade anything this old world has to offer for them."

Silence lingered between Brad and Kara, both conscious of his words, touched by his sentiment, stung by their own lack of it.

"Now I want you two to enjoy this hot tub," Erastus continued. "I expect it to get a lot of good use."

Visions of hot bubbling water and naked skin emerged and Kara and Brad glanced away from each other.

"Never know when I'll make another surprise inspection," Erastus warned.

"It'll get used," Brad promised as he glanced pointedly at Kara. Ignoring her startled look, he gestured toward the busy crew of men. "This is very generous of you, Erastus. But I could swear the spa wasn't listed in the original contract."

Kara walked away to take a closer glance at the tub.

Erastus shrugged, the twinkle in his eye doing a merry dance. "Might be you had more on your mind than facts and figures that day."

Remembering the role he was playing, Brad returned Erastus's smile, trying not to let the strain show. "Could be."

"Hell, love's like a roller coaster ride, son. Some of the time you're soaring so high, you'd swear you're flying. Other times you think the whole thing's going to make you sick. But at the end of the ride, you wouldn't give up the experience for anything."

Glancing over at Kara, Brad felt the strange tugging feeling that never quite left him. While each day now brought more surprises than he'd ever thought possible, the nights remained a sweet torture, one he wasn't certain he could endure. Nor one he was prepared to relinquish.

That truth hit him much like the roller coaster Erastus had just mentioned—and the track was on a straight course to his gut. Another thought struck him.

Maybe he'd been taking the wrong tack in their arrangement. Instead of torturing himself, perhaps he should try to end the agony. Instead of spending the nights wondering how it could be, perhaps he should find out.

So, instead of antagonizing her, maybe he ought to try a little old-fashioned seduction.

Kara turned just then, her golden hair glinting in the early-morning sunshine. She was dressed simply, as always, in a pink T-shirt that hugged her skin, as did the faded jeans she wore. But on her the combination was more alluring than satin and lace, and Brad felt their effect like an iron hammer pounding against his senses.

"Lost you again, didn't I, son?" Erastus grinned as he spoke.

Realizing that he'd tuned out the older man, Brad returned his attention to their conversation. "Sorry. Daydreaming."

Erastus followed the direction of Brad's gaze. "Can't say as I blame you. Nope, not one bit."

GLEAMING FIBERGLASS and the scent of new lumber filled the deck area. Competent workmen had the installation completed in record time. What had seemed like a big job surprisingly hadn't taken long at all. Now filled with fresh water and the required additives, the hot tub simmered beneath the growing dusk, sending out a sensual message that Brad intended to fulfill.

But first he had to convince Kara. Luckily her mother and Chuck had left already for an early dinner. Which left the scene of the crime ready.

Passing through the living room, he saw that she'd managed to move his chair out of sight again. If it didn't seem so ridiculous, it would be funny. He grinned in spite of himself. It was hard to get mad when she was so creative about hiding his favorite recliner.

Last time he'd found it in the storeroom behind the garage. Not certain how she'd managed to lug it that far, he had to give her points for originality. As his glance fell on the sofa table, his grin turned into a look of surprise. So far she hadn't moved any of his collectibles. And they were all still there, including the shrunken head. But his goddess of fertility had a new addition.

Stepping closer, he fingered the scarf she'd fashioned into a dress to cover the nude figurine. The goddess no longer looked seductive. No, it was downright sedate.

It appeared Kara had been on modesty patrol while he'd been busy plotting ways to lower her barriers. Deliberately shoving aside the thought, instead he concentrated on some originality of his own.

KARA SWORE as she stumbled through the darkened hallway, planning to strangle Brad when she found him. Cute trick, taking all of her clothes from the closet except her bathing suit. She couldn't even find her scruffy terry-cloth robe. He was thorough.

And he was going to pay.

But first she had to navigate through the house. Apparently the electricity was out. Candles had been lit and placed in strategic places. But the house was hardly aglow. Instead, the candlelight flickered, giving off only dim illumination. She'd planned on grabbing something to eat since she was starving, having skipped lunch, as well as dinner, but first she was going to find Brad.

Reaching the study, she saw that the French doors stood open. Passing through them, she was startled to see a bottle of champagne resting in an ice bucket atop the patio table. The gentle roar of the hot tub bubbled nearby, and from the darkness Brad emerged, clad only in a pair of swimming trunks.

He held out a pair of matched wineglasses, but she stared at them without reaching for the one he offered.

"*You* did this?" She gestured back to the candle-lit house and then at her bathing suit.

"I thought we ought to christen our newest acquisition."

"Funny, you didn't go to this much trouble when we got our first flock of new birds."

He held his smile in place, but Kara detected a tick of annoyance. Good.

"I could go get them and see if they'd like to take a dip with us," he offered.

"Asking them first would be more notice than I got," she responded sweetly, referring to his "clothesnapping."

"This way you don't have to come up with a thousand reasons why we have to keep everything businesslike."

"I didn't know I needed any reasons," she responded, wishing he'd go put on a shirt and jeans. The expanse of bare male skin made her throat go dry and her stomach tighten nervously. Her gaze continued to dwell on the beguiling swirl of hair on his chest that trailed over a flattened abdomen to disappear somewhere beneath his navel.

Every night she'd wondered about the man sharing her bed, but she'd studiously kept to her own side, sometimes scarcely sleeping as she kept her rigid control in place. But even in her now highly active dreams, she hadn't imagined standing next to him clad only in a swimsuit, while he looked so... so enticing. Having only sneaked occasional glances at him while he was clad in his boxers, she couldn't help staring at him now. Her stomach somersaulted, landing in a tight wedge somewhere near her breastbone.

He shrugged, lifting a muscled shoulder as her eyes followed its silhouette. "I can't help but notice you always have a multitude of reasons on hand."

Kara swallowed, purposely glancing away from him toward a fascinating spot somewhere near her big toe. "There's no need to be so dramatic about the tub. I like a good soak myself." She took one of the glasses of champagne and quickly downed it, immediately holding it out for a refill.

He complied as surprise etched itself over his face. Then he eased out a half grin, which managed to look incredibly sexy. Why couldn't she have a business partner that looked like Harpo Marx instead of the hunk-of-the-month?

Easing into the tub, she welcomed the warmth as she turned to him. "The candles are pretty inventive. But when did the electricity go out? It was still on when I was in the shower, but as soon as I got dressed, everything went dark."

Rather than answering, Brad refilled her glass of champagne, which she drank without comment, determined not to act like a prude. Apparently she'd been doing a lot of that, for him to go to such lengths simply to get her to share their new hot tub. Since their living arrangements obviously hadn't gotten to him, she needed to relax, just take things as casually as he did.

Drinking the champagne faster than she normally would, Kara felt a faint buzz. Ignoring it, she held out her glass for more. Seeing the surprise on Brad's face before he refilled the glass, she waved her other hand in the frothing water. "Bubbly for the bubbles."

"Uh-huh. Look, I wouldn't drink that quite so fast...."

But she'd already emptied the fourth glass and refilled it. The buzz was growing. "Aren't you going to join me?" Was that her voice, all throaty and dark?

Shoving the champagne bottle and his own still-full glass out of reach, Brad slid into the water. Mesmerized, she watched the moist droplets caress his skin and found she wanted to do the same.

"You shouldn't drink much when you're in a hot tub," he cautioned. "It's too easy to pass out and drown."

"But you wouldn't let me drown, would you?" she purred, trailing the tips of her fingernails over his chest. His pecs twitched and she could see a battle waging across his face.

"Did you have anything to eat tonight?"

She studied the question, trying to remember, but everything seemed fuzzy. Even her recent hunger and missed meals were forgotten. "Dunno. Did you?"

He sighed. "Maybe we should grab something to eat before it gets any later and you get...well, before it gets any later."

"I'm not hungry," she replied, inching closer to him. Unable to resist, she moved her hands through his hair that now curled in the warm mist of the bubbling water. She'd always liked his hair, so dark, thick and rich. With a lock of his hair twirled around her finger, she moved the other hand toward his face, tracing the outline of his lips. "At least I'm not hungry for food."

"You're not thinking clearly," he said, sounding strangulated.

"How do you know? You can't see inside my head." She tilted her head, loving the feel of his strong shoulder beside her. "My brain might be a dark cola, or I could be Crystal Light."

"You could be smashed," he muttered, moving away slightly.

Kara floated back toward him, erasing the distance. "Now, is that what you say to all the ladies? Surely you can think of a smoother line."

His sigh was heartfelt. "You'd think so. Okay, it's time to get out." Not giving her a choice, he lifted her from the water and, holding her, stepped out of the tub.

"Are we done?" she asked as the cool night air met her wet skin.

"I'm afraid so," he replied grimly.

"Don't you want to tub with me anymore?" Kara could hear the entreaty in her voice, but wanted to recapture the pleasant feeling she'd experienced while in the water with him.

"Another time. Right now, I think you'd better take a nap."

She twined her hands around his neck. "Are you sleepy, too? Lucky we have a big bed."

His voice was gruff. "No, this is a solo flight."

"Too bad. We could share."

"That's what I thought. Apparently it was a bad plan." Pausing at the breaker box, he flipped a switch before entering the house, which seemed unnaturally bright as all the lights she'd turned on while stumbling in the dark now blazed.

"The lights work now," she commented, feeling safe and protected in his strong arms.

"So they do." He moved through the hall and into the master suite, laying her on the bed. Drawing up a comforter, his hands lingered for a moment, finally smoothing her hair.

"You're nice," she murmured. "Most men aren't this nice."

A pang shot across his face and she vaguely wondered about it before her eyelids flickered closed. "Real nice."

Brad continued to stare at her, but she was already drifting to sleep. So much for his plan to seduce her. Right now he felt like the world's biggest jerk.

Turning off the lights, he left the door ajar as he moved into the other room, absently turning off the wealth of lights that now shone obscenely. Snuffing the candles, he collected them, not wanting her to see the evidence of his stupidity.

Once in the kitchen, he dumped the entire mess into the garbage can. Leaning against the kitchen counter, he stared outside at the pool and hot tub area. What had seemed like a good idea had done more than backfire on him. It was a cold splashing reminder that he'd undertaken a business arrangement with Kara. Nothing else.

Purposely he tried to dismiss the memory of her long, shapely legs that seemed to go on forever. Even though her suit was a modest, one-piece affair, it hugged those curves he was so aware of each night. What's more, she seemed unaware of her stunning looks. It was enchanting, entrancing, and not a little bit maddening.

If she was one of the women he was used to, the ones who spent as much time in front of the mirror as they did flirting, Kara would be easy to dismiss. Instead, she was fresh and different.

Dangerously different.

Because she held half the title to *his* ranch. And if they messed up, as they'd almost done in front of Erastus that morning, they would lose the ranch.

Jamming his hands into his pockets, Brad strolled to the French doors and outside. If he closed his eyes, he could imagine the ranch as it must have been a hundred years ago, filled with taciturn ranch hands and the bawling sounds of milling cattle.

Even though he was in a high-tech industry, Brad felt a kinship with the land, its unchanging place in history. Now that he actually owned the ranch, the place was even more important to him, digging deep into his soul. Gazing into the sky that remained unfettered and endless, he could imagine ranchers of other eras doing much the same thing, gauging the weather for the next cattle drive, or wondering at the loneliness of such a vast land.

Glancing at the darkened bedroom window, Brad thought of the woman who lay there, one who could end that loneliness. And one who could also cause him to lose this piece of his dream. From the first time he'd ridden on horseback over the Rocking J, he'd known. The love of the ranch was as much a part of him as the dark ebony of his eyes.

It had always seemed out of reach until now. But he wondered suddenly if they could last out the remainder of their fast disappearing time, sharing a house.

And a bed.

Nightingales stirred the quiet, reminding him that Muriel would return that evening. Even though he didn't want to test his control by sleeping in the same room with Kara, he couldn't bunk in the study without giving up the charade. And it was important to Kara that her mother not find out.

He wondered suddenly when what mattered to Kara had become important to him. Shaking his head, he refused to give the thought credit. It was just his frustration talking. Especially when he had to keep a careful distance from Kara.

It had been a damn fool idea to think he could seduce her and then occupy the same house with her afterward. Abandoning that plan was the only thing that made sense. But the aching tightness of his body reminded him that logic was talking. And it was acting alone. Because his body had zoned in on Kara's nearness.

Even though she was peacefully sleeping, her allure didn't diminish. He imagined how the night might have ended if he'd ignored the effects of the champagne and taken advantage of her inebriation. The further tightening of his body convinced him to abandon that train of thought. Before the engine ran him over.

KARA STRETCHED, immediately feeling the emptiness of the bed. She wondered if Brad had risen early to tend the ostriches. Sitting up abruptly, she clutched her head as it reacted to the sudden movement, seeming to scream in protest.

What in the world?

But her pain was diverted by the sight of Brad sprawled out on the vanity chair by the window. His long frame was cramped into a pretzel-shaped position by the uncomfortable chair he slept in. Narrowing her eyes, she wondered what would have forced him to sleep in that torture trap. She grabbed the sheet and blanket, pulling them back so she could get out of bed.

Startled, she simply stared at the bathing suit she wore. Dimly a blurry memory of the previous evening floated in her hazy mind. She vaguely remembered the hot tub. But why had she climbed into bed still wearing her suit?

Purposely remaining quiet, she eased out of bed and stepped carefully past Brad. Walking to the closet, she automatically grabbed for her robe and came up empty-handed. She peered inside and saw more air, but no clothes. Her head pounded in accompaniment to her confusion and the harder she tried to figure out what had happened, the more the pain intensified.

An examination of her dresser came up empty, as well. One thing was certain. She couldn't remain in her bathing suit. And the only clothes in the room were Brad's. Choosing one of his T-shirts, she stumbled into the adjoining bath, thinking a shower might clear her head. She stripped off her suit and, stepping beneath the pounding spray, hoped the water would dislodge the cobwebs in her brain. Though her head wasn't any clearer, she found relief from the aching headache as the spiking water massaged her neck and shoulders.

Dunking her hair beneath the water, she relished the feel of the spray as it soothed her aching scalp. Not bothering to be quiet, she allowed the water to continue its therapeutic assault. But hearing noises in the bedroom over the sound of the shower, she reached up to turn off the water.

Not wanting to meet Brad head-on in the bathroom and admit that she'd lost all of her clothes, she grabbed a towel. Hearing him come closer, she dropped the towel and whipped the T-shirt over her head. When the bathroom door opened, she was breathing hard whether from exertion or anticipation she wasn't sure.

Water from her hair dripped down the shirt, flattening the thin cotton against her breasts, rendering it transparent. Seeing his gaze fasten on the trail of moisture, her nipples hardened in response.

The heat from his gaze traveled to her, igniting a similar reaction. Aware of her bare legs, scarcely skimmed by the T-shirt, she felt exposed, somewhat wanton, and the hunger in his look gave rise to a forbidden pleasure at causing that hunger.

But abruptly he stepped back, jerking his gaze away. "I didn't know you were in here," he explained lamely.

She pressed a hand against her sopping hair. "I was just going to do my hair, but I won't be long."

"Take your time. I'll use the other bathroom," he muttered, slamming the door in record time. The noise ricocheted through her head and she looked longingly back at the shower.

Giving in to the temptation, she stripped off the sodden shirt and dove back into the shower. When she'd almost exhausted all the hot water, she emerged. Blinking, she saw her terry robe hanging on the back of the door. She decided she must have just overlooked it. Grateful for its protective folds, she donned it and then blow-dried her hair.

After applying a touch of makeup she reentered the bedroom. With a sigh, she realized she still hadn't located her clothes. Walking to the closet, she opened it to see if she could raid something else of Brad's. But she blinked again. All of her clothes hung neatly in place again.

The nagging pain at her temples throbbed with new life. Maybe she'd flipped. Quitting a solid job, trying to start a new business, a marriage of convenience to someone she didn't really know, carrying on the charade for her mother. Maybe it was all too much. Was a stop at the rubber room next?

Gingerly she reached for a shirt and jeans, hoping they wouldn't turn to fairy dust in her hands. Since they were reassuringly solid, she laid them on the bed and reached automatically into the dresser drawer that held her bras and panties. It too should have been empty. But it wasn't.

This was getting spooky.

Hurriedly she dressed, and as she was snapping her jeans, Brad pounded on the bedroom door. "You decent?"

Clutching her head at the renewed assault on her tender nerve endings, Kara sank to the bed before calling out weakly. "You can come in." As an afterthought, she glanced at him as he walked in, lowering her voice to a whisper. "Where's my mother?"

"Outside. I remember the rules." *Or at least he thought he had.* "Look, about last night—"

"Not so loud, okay?" Flinching, she massaged both temples. "What about last night? I don't remember a thing."

He sucked in his breath, but she was too concerned with the pounding in her head. "Nothing at all?"

"Something about a hot tub... I think." She started to meet his gaze, then shifted her glance away. "Maybe I've been trying to take on too much all at once. You know—the job, the ranch, our... business arrangement."

"What makes you say that?" he asked, noting the pallor beneath her eyes. With a jolt of surprise he studied her face, beginning to realize the extent of her hangover.

"I don't know," she hedged. "But I think I'll skip today's auction."

"The pairs I traded the breeder for should arrive today or tomorrow," he answered, watching her for signs of a sudden memory gain.

She waved a hand. "Fine. I'll just be hanging out here. If the truck comes, I'll take the delivery."

"Even if you have to let them out of the truck?"

Already pale, she managed to turn an even unhealthier shade. Surprising him, she gathered her scattered strength. "Sure, no problem."

Right. She didn't look capable of unloading a truckload of goldfish. "I don't have to go to the auction, either," he remarked casually. "I'll wait for the delivery." And see if she regained any of her memory about the previous evening.

"You don't have to stick around—"

"There's another auction next week in Fort Worth. We should both go. It'll be a pretty big investment."

She wasn't difficult to convince. Arguing just made her head pound harder. "Okay. Do you know where the aspirin is?"

He kept his grin in check. "Headache?"

She waved her hand dismissively as she climbed unsteadily to her feet. "I just need my coffee."

"Bacon and eggs?"

She pressed one hand to her lips, her face paling even more. "I don't think so."

Deciding he'd pushed his luck far enough, Brad backed off. "I'll meet you on the patio."

Gathering the coffee and croissants, Brad waited near the edge of the pool. Grimly he wondered if she'd have instant recall when she stepped outside.

Kara walked carefully from the house as though the ground were covered in fragile eggshells. Squinting as the sunlight hit her eyes, she ducked quickly beneath the umbrella covering at the table.

"Coffee?"

She jumped, then tried to cover the motion. "Thanks." Taking the cup, she added cream and drank the coffee greedily. "I needed that. I feel about a quart low."

She looked it, too, but he wasn't about to say so.

Lowering the cup, she glanced quizzically at the hot tub. Expecting recognition to dawn, he held his breath. But her face cleared as she turned back to him.

"Nice of Erastus to have the tub delivered. Seems like he could have gotten a credit on it."

"Yeah, he's a real decent guy."

She stared at her cup for a moment, then at him. His gut tightened.

"Do we have any more coffee?" she asked finally.

At this rate, he'd have a heart attack trying to decide if she was going to remember. "I'll get the carafe."

She nodded, staring off in the direction of the hot tub as he brought more coffee to the table.

"You know... I was thinking..." she began.

This was it.

"A cabana would be nice."

"Excuse me?"

"One of those built-in places to change next to the pool." She gripped her mug, thinking about waking up in her bathing suit. "For guests, I mean."

"Croissant?"

She shook her head violently, then looked as though she regretted the action. "No... I'm not hungry."

They both heard the humming at the same time. It was Muriel in the garden. It occurred to Brad that it was time to have that talk with Chuck before his friend's relationship with Muriel grew any deeper. This charade had gone from difficult to near impossible. He didn't need Chuck adding to his irritation, and the past few days he'd stirred things up as much as possible. Besides, he didn't want a nice woman like Muriel hurt. Chuck was his friend, but Kara had been right in her original assessment. Chuck wasn't the steady type.

"I hope she stays in the garden," Kara murmured as she watched Muriel carry her basket of freshly cut flowers through the winding rows of the azaleas and roses.

"Not into socializing this morning?"

"I love her to death but sometimes she sees too much."

His thought exactly.

"I dreamed the strangest thing," she said.

Brad held his breath.

"The whole house was lit by candles." She hugged her coffee, warming her fingers against the mug. "It was kind of nice."

He exhaled.

"You were there," she continued.

Choking on the coffee he'd just swallowed, he grabbed for a napkin.

"Hey, you okay, Brad?" Concerned, she bent forward to pat him on the back.

This was too much. Certain he was about to be struck dead, Brad rose and stepped away. Gulping back the cough rumbling in his chest, he nodded. Muriel was walking closer, her humming filling the air.

"I'm fine. Look, I need to head out to the airport and talk to Chuck."

"Oh, okay." Sinking back into her chair, she reached for her coffee. "Just another cup and I'll be back to myself."

And cows fly. "Right. The delivery truck won't be here until afternoon. I'll be back before then."

CHUCK FILED THE flight plan as Brad impatiently waited for the right opportunity to discuss Muriel with him. He'd just finished altering the schedule, assigning Chuck as many flights as possible so that he wouldn't have much time to see Muriel.

Last night's fiasco in the hot tub hovered in Brad's mind. It was clear he needed to eliminate all the complications he could, starting with Chuck. His friend was a ladies' man and it had occurred to Brad that he was doing Muriel a favor, as well. He'd grown fond of her and didn't want to see her hurt.

Even though Chuck was technically an employee, Brad could hardly order him to back off. Chuck would tell him to fly his airplane to geographically impossible places, which he'd done enough times in the past.

"So, what brings you out to the hangar so early?" Chuck asked, slinging a leather backpack over his shoulder as they headed toward the plane.

Brad considered dancing around the reason, then discarded the notion. "It's about you and Muriel."

Chuck stopped and turned toward Brad. "Something happen to Muriel?"

Hearing the concern lacing his friend's words, Brad hesitated. "Not exactly."

"Then what? *Exactly!*"

"Don't get so excited. Last time I saw her she was gardening—humming a lot."

Chuck visibly relaxed. "Then what do you want to talk about?"

"I want to know how you feel about her."

"Don't you think that's absolutely none of your business?" Chuck responded without a bit of malice.

"Not so. She is my mother-in-law."

Chuck laughed, a deep throaty sound. "Yeah. Don't forget who knows the truth behind that." His eyes narrowed suddenly. "Or is that what this is all about? Trying to run me off so I won't let on to Muriel about why you two really got married?"

Brad hid the truth of Chuck's accurate guess. "Kara's concerned about her mother."

Chuck eyed him suspiciously. "Why?"

"Because she's never dated anyone since her husband died."

Disbelief flitted across Chuck's face. "But it's been almost ten years!"

"Kara's point exactly. And let's face it. You're not the most serious guy in the world. Kara's afraid Muriel's going to fall for you. Then you'll do your usual it was nice, babe, act, and she'll be crushed."

Chuck didn't reply. It was clear his thoughts were miles away.

"Look, man. I don't want to spoil your fun, but Muriel's not your normal type."

Chuck stared into the distance, his words drawn out slowly. "No... she's not."

Brad clapped a hand around Chuck's shoulder, vaguely disturbed by Chuck's reaction. It was what he wanted, but still... "Hey, it's not like you won't be seeing her. She'll be at the ranch till her house gets fixed, which looks like it could be months.''

"Yeah . . . right."

"I only want what's best for her," Brad added, suddenly not sure that was what he'd accomplished. Definitely sure it hadn't been his true purpose.

Chuck met his gaze, the usual devilment missing in his eyes. "You don't need to tell me, Brad. I know I'm not ideal husband material." He hitched up his backpack. "Look, I've got to get going. Takeoff's in a few minutes."

As he strode away, Brad stared after him in shock. *Husband material?* Where had that come from? Could he have just put a bomb in a genuine relationship, blowing it to smithereens while it was still growing?

Suddenly his brilliant idea seemed like the dumbest thing he'd ever done. Correction, the second dumbest thing. The first was thinking he could carry out this entire charade.

Chapter Eight

Kara snuggled closer into the warmth. This was her best dream ever...it seemed so real. As she splayed her hands over the solid width of Brad's chest, she could imagine that the flesh beneath her fingers was almost real. Along with the swirl of silken hair, the sculpted muscles that played beneath the skin, the strength she sensed there. Sighing, she eased deeper into her dream.

She could feel Brad's strength, sense his fingers dancing over her skin. She throbbed with the sensation of what those fingers would do to her, how they would ply against her skin, tantalizing, fulfilling.

Chest-to-chest, hipbone-to-hipbone, the warmth intensified as their legs wound together.

Sleepily Kara opened her eyes.

And met Brad's unblinking stare.

She froze, her lips parted. No sound emerged. But Brad remained silent, as well.

Kara was so close to him she could easily trace the laughter lines near his eyes, see the sweep of dark lashes so luxuriant most women would kill for them. His nostrils flared as one lip edged upward. Her scant silk nightgown was little protection against the length of his body. For all intents and purposes, they could be naked beneath the down quilt.

And that realization brought her back to reality as she whipped her legs from his and bolted backward in the bed. At her movement, Brad jerked away until they each occupied separate sides of the bed.

Sunshine streamed in the oversize bay window, lighting the room. It was difficult to hide the truth in such stark daylight. Tension rose as rapidly as the sun that climbed in the East.

Kara was the first to break the standoff. "I need the bathroom first." Grabbing her robe, she darted toward the bathroom. She knew it was a cowardly move, but she took refuge in the four sturdy walls that surrounded her, listening until she heard Brad leave the bedroom.

Grabbing a muffin and a glass of orange juice, Kara didn't wait around to see if Brad was in the house. Instead she fled toward the door. But as she rounded the corner, she saw Aunt Tillie peeking at her from the laundry room where she'd stuck the portrait after its last abduction. She hadn't had time to let Brad know she'd found the picture. Reaching out, she grasped the painting as a grin formed, shoving aside her earlier butterflies. There was more than one way to skin a hardheaded man.

KARA PUSHED Brad's ancient recliner behind the saddles in the tack room. It was the same place she'd found Aunt Tillie after Brad had stashed the picture in retaliation for her last move of his chair. She doubted he would think to look in the same place.

At least not for a while.

Flexing her arms, Kara realized she was getting a better workout than when she spent five days a week at the gym in town. And it was a lot more fun.

Aunt Tillie grinned lopsidedly from her sideways position in the hay on the floor. Kara carefully dusted her off and righted the picture. Brad seemed willing to carry on the hide-and-seek game as long as she did. She'd thought he would have been upset to find the dress she'd fashioned to cover his sensual goddess of fertility. Instead, unperturbed, he'd added a dashing beret, making her feel rather foolish.

Clutching the picture under her arm, Kara emerged from the room behind the barn. As she cleared the stable area, she saw a truck parked out front. The delivery.

It hadn't come the previous day or the one before when she'd felt so ghastly. Now, fully recovered, she was anxious to see the pairs Brad had traded for.

Looking around, she found a suitable hiding spot in the grain bin next to the stable doors. She slid Aunt Tillie inside, silently apologizing for the indignity. But it would hardly do to let Brad know she'd found the picture so easily.

Striding over to the truck, she saw Brad smiling with pleasure.

"This driver's from the breeder," he announced confidently. "Since he hauls around ostriches on a regular basis, he'll let the birds into the pen."

She shrugged, trying to appear disinterested in his superior method of getting the birds delivered. Who would think to ask if the driver unloaded the birds? Only Brad, who, as usual, had planned this down to the last detail, unlike her helter-skelter delivery.

He hadn't forgotten for a moment that she didn't have the experience he'd expected. In truth it was a wonder they hadn't blown the operation apart—two novices, each thinking the other was the expert. Luck alone had kept them afloat, that and the well-timed appearances from Erastus, who was always willing to give them seasoned advice when needed.

If two people could be more opposite in every way, she didn't know how. Brad always planned ahead. Mr. Methodical. Forget impulse. She slanted a glance at him from beneath her eyelashes, wondering if he ever gave in to the moment. This morning, for example... it could have had a very different outcome.

Certainly he hadn't seemed inclined to dislodge the barriers between them. No, straight on course. Always thinking of the ranch, never of her. She wondered why that stung so.

Watching the van back up to the corral, then the driver opening the door, she expected to see that in typical Brad fashion, these would be the best birds they'd seen yet.

The door opened, the ramp was flung down and she heard the clatter of hooves. The birds were everything she'd expected.

Except for one minor detail.

Holding her smirk in check, she tilted her head as she watched his smug smile, anticipating its demise.

"Nice stock, Brad."

"Sure is," he agreed, still grinning.

"So these are the pairs you traded for?" she continued in an even tone, savoring the moment.

"Yep. It took a lot of *planning* but it was worth it."

"Uh-huh." She circled the van, pausing near the opened back ramp. She was glad that Brad walked along beside her. Revenge was sweet. "Did the breeder happen to mention how male pairs were going to breed?"

His smile slowly dissolved as he stared around the corral, seeing the distinctive black plumage of the male birds, recognition dawning. "Where the heck are the females?"

She couldn't resist. "Good question."

"Maybe they're in the back of the van—"

"Empty."

"Then there's been a mistake."

"Did you specify the kind of pairs you wanted, Brad?"

"Pairs are supposed to be mated pairs, Kara. Any dimwit would know that."

She smiled sweetly. "You didn't. Unmated pairs come in both sexes. Pairs of males, pairs of females, or one of each. You were supposed to ask for proven *mated laying* pairs. I don't want to speak rashly, but I'd just about bet the ranch that's not what you got."

Stalking forward, he stared at the distinctly male birds, the muscles in his clenched jaw twitching dangerously. "I planned so well."

"I never did cotton much to plans."

"I've noticed," he muttered.

"What?" she asked sharply.

But he shook his head. "I can't believe this. And something tells me the breeder won't take back another shipment in trade."

"Then take them to auction," she suggested impulsively.

"But we haven't made any plans...."

She cocked an eyebrow at him. "Make a few phone calls, Brad. Go with the flow or stick with your flow chart. Because we either take them to auction or we're stuck with them until we do a lot of selling and trading.''

He muttered something unintelligible, but Kara could guess his meaning. He walked toward the house and she could hear fragments of his continued soliloquy. "Damn birds... *pairs!*"

Smiling, she went to retrieve Aunt Tillie, looking forward to the next round.

STEPPING INTO THE hotel room, Brad allowed the bellman to flick on the lights.

"Sorry about the suite, sir. But with the airport fogged in, all the rooms are full. Management thought it was only right to split up the suites, so everyone could have a place to sleep. Hope you and your wife don't mind."

Kara smiled weakly. It seemed almost more intimate to be sharing a bedroom in a hotel than at the ranch. Here there was the wicked freedom of anonymity. And coming to the stupid auction had been *her* idea. At least bringing their own birds, which had forced them to come a day early.

The bellman pointed toward the corner of the room. "We did make sure you got one of the rooms with a hot tub, though. Hope it'll make up for losing the suite." He pointed toward an iced champagne bucket on the table. "Compliments of the management. Hope you have a good stay."

Brad pulled out a bill and offered it to the man.

"Thank you, sir. Ring if you need anything else."

Purposely averting his gaze from the champagne bucket and the hot tub, hoping they didn't trigger any memories for Kara, Brad opened the closet. "Plenty of space."

"Uh-huh." But Kara had walked to the balcony, staring at the magnificent display the city below provided. "This is wonderful." Lights winked at them, seeming to spread out for miles as the duo cities of Dallas and Fort Worth themselves did.

"Hungry? This city has some of the finest restaurants in the world."

"Hmm?" She turned back to him. "Yes, I'd like some dinner. But let me change first, okay?"

His eyes were fastened on her face. She looked wonderful to him, but he nodded, glancing down at his own attire.

"First dibs on the bathroom," she said quickly, acting on pure feminine instinct.

He grinned at her. The hotel setting created an atmosphere they hadn't experienced before. A totally male-female situation. One they were both succumbing to. One that made him want to be gallant. And to forget the animosity that simmered between them.

Away from the pressures they faced daily, it seemed natural to defer to her. "I'll be on the balcony."

"Feasting on the stars," she suggested glibly.

But he didn't have an equally glib response. Because he could take to just such a notion. Especially if she was part of that feast. "Take your time."

And she did. Glancing at his watch, he realized an hour had passed. He wondered what could be taking her so long.

"Brad?" Her voice was soft, questioning.

Glancing up, he felt her presence like a blow. Soft black silk billowed around her like a midnight cloud. Her shoulders were bared by the dipping neckline; her golden hair a stunning contrast against the jet black of the dress. Her smile was tentative. "Is this too dressy? You mentioned a fine restaurant. . . ."

He cleared his throat. "No. You look perfect." And she did.

The smile grew along with an arch look in her eyes. "Did I take too long?"

Not as long as she looked like that. He could have waited a dozen hours and it would have been worth it.

His voice was husky, despite his efforts to sound normal. "No. I'll just be a minute." Inside, he shaved, then dashed into the shower. Digging quickly through his garment bag for something appropriate, he was amazed to find his charcoal gray suit, a starched white shirt and cuff links. Things he hadn't packed.

"Kara must have done this, the little minx," he muttered with a growing smile. Grateful that she'd included all the right accessories, he dressed quickly. Glancing in the mirror to comb his hair, he wondered at her motives. Then decided he hoped they were completely lascivious.

He stepped back on the balcony and drew in his breath as he saw Kara silhouetted against the midnight-colored backdrop of sky and stars. Allowing himself to drink in her appearance, he wondered if he should be locked up for not realizing what a truly exquisite woman she was. She turned as she heard his approach, the green of her eyes going all smoky.

"You look very handsome," she murmured.

Realizing he hadn't commented on her appearance, he held out a hand. "Couldn't escort the most beautiful woman in town wearing jeans and a T-shirt."

Surprise flickered over her fine-boned features. "I believe the night air has gotten to you, Brad Holbrook."

"Something has," he said beneath his breath.

She cocked her head, unable to make out the words, so he smiled instead.

"Our carriage awaits," he said, taking her arm.

"Carriage?"

"Okay, a yellow cab, but use your imagination."

She laughed as they left the room and stepped into the elevator. The other people in the elevator glanced at them, seeing a handsome man and a beautiful woman. The perfect couple.

Downstairs, Brad excused himself and headed for the concierge, hoping the man could wrangle reservations at a decent restaurant. Outlining his problem, Brad was relieved to see the man nod his head.

"I think we can arrange something, sir. Your name?"

"Holbrook. I'm in Room 1912."

The concierge scratched his forehead as a puzzled look crossed his face. "But I made those reservations for you, sir. Your table will be waiting for you."

Brad stared at the other man. Had Kara... "Did my wife..."

"No, sir. It was the older, white-haired gentleman who set everything up. In fact, your limo's out front."

Brad considered looking this gift horse in the mouth then decided against it. If fate had decided to hand him a limo and world-class reservations, he wasn't bucking it. Instead he rewarded the messenger of his good news with a hefty tip. Kara looked suitably impressed when Brad ushered her into the white stretch limo. Music played softly and a full bar tempted them.

"Brad, this is wonderful. I never expected anything like this!" Her eyes shone and he caught her excitement, even though he managed a nonchalant shrug.

The dark night whooshed by as the driver navigated through the considerable traffic. Brad poured them both glasses of a delightful chardonnay.

Kara swirled the liquid in her glass. "Where are we eating, Brad?"

He nearly choked on the wine he was sipping.

When he didn't answer immediately, she dropped her lashes coyly. "It's not a dark, mysterious secret, is it?"

Was it ever. "I..." He glanced up, seeing that the car was sliding into the curb next to the restaurant's bright, flared canopy. He could scarcely hide his relief. "We're here. Wasn't a surprise better?"

She was subdued as they entered the restaurant known for its elegant intimacy. Strains of the string quartet stirred softly in the air, unobtrusive but provoking. The maître d' escorted them to a table by the window, overlooking the provocative lights of the city.

"If the food's as good as the atmosphere, I applaud your choice," Kara said as she studied the menu.

"Better than tacos and Chinese takeout," he assured her, meeting her gaze, hoping she didn't call his bluff.

Instead the remembered meal on their wedding night dashed them both into a wave of memories.

Kara cleared her throat. "I'm sure it will be good."

"Rack of lamb for two?" the waiter suggested.

"Does that come in pairs?" Kara asked as she glanced down at her menu and then met the answering smile in Brad's eyes.

The waiter offered a few more suggestions, took their order, then brought a bottle of wine. Kara drank conservatively, only sipping at the excellent vintage.

Brad was relieved, knowing he didn't want a repeat performance of the champagne and hot tub escapade. No, he wanted Kara willing.

The thought rocked him. Especially when it was clear she hadn't shown an iota of interest in him. Oh, she'd tried to be noncombative lately, but that was all.

Longing seeped through him as he watched Kara's elegant posture, the beguiling profile and those captivating eyes. If he'd handled things differently, they might not still be polite strangers, sharing only a business.

But he didn't intend to pursue any more elaborate plans to seduce her. He'd learned that the best laid plans were apparently the ones to backfire in the worst way.

Brad held up his wineglass. "To a profitable partnership."

Something he couldn't define flickered in her eyes. But she held up her glass and clicked it together with his. She hesitated before drawing the glass back, then tipped it to her lips and took a swallow. The warmth in his stomach curled as he watched the curve of her mouth, remembering the feel of it beneath his lips, wanting desperately to take another taste.

The attentive waiter brought steaming bowls of soup, ending the moment. Kept supplied with several courses of delicious dishes, they were occupied by the food and service until they finished the coffee.

"Dessert?" the waiter asked.

Kara shook her head regretfully. "I couldn't."

"I think that will be all. It was an excellent meal," Brad added.

"Thank you, sir." After clearing the dishes, the waiter discreetly left them alone.

"I'd like to get to the stockyard early," Brad said as he replaced his coffee cup. "Make sure the birds got there okay."

"Good idea."

An awkward silence descended as they realized they had to return to the hotel room alone. She laughed awkwardly.

"This is silly. It's just one night."

"Right."

But the strain continued as they rode back in the cab. The ride seemed far shorter this time and the hotel loomed up beside them in no time. Brad considered suggesting a drink in the hotel bar, but thought better of it. He didn't want to get her smashed again. Even though logically he knew she hadn't eaten the other time and had drunk too much, far too fast, he didn't want to set up the same situation.

This time the elevator ride up to the room seemed closed in, tense. Too soon they were in their room.

Kara paced nervously toward the balcony, flinging her clutch purse onto the table. The large room diminished, pressing in on them both.

Turning to look at Brad, Kara's glance fell on the bed, dismay and anxiety filling her face. "I know," she said brightly, hoping to stall the moment when she had to climb into that bed beside him. "Why don't we get in the hot tub for a while?"

He blanched. It was like a bad dream. One that wouldn't go away. While he'd like nothing better than to share a hot tub of water with her dressed in as little as possible, he didn't want to risk having her remember his botched plan at the ranch. And he wasn't stupid enough to think that plan could somehow work this time.

"I don't know. It's late..."

"Please?"

Hearing the entreaty in her voice, he sighed. After all, he could restrain himself then suggest they get out quickly before she remembered anything. "Okay. But just for a little while. I really have to get up early."

Kara smiled in relief. "I'll change in the bathroom."

He nodded, reaching for his garment bag. He hoped she didn't have instant recall and try to drown him.

But her face didn't betray anything as she emerged from the bathroom. He hoped his didn't, either. Because she looked even better than he remembered. Those legs might be his undoing yet.

Clearing his throat, he gestured for her to get in the tub first. Following her in from behind, he wasn't sure that was such a good idea. She looked as good from the rear.

Kara let the bubbles surround her and realized this was a really dumb idea. And a rotten way to kill time. If Brad unnerved her fully clothed, devastatingly handsome in his tailored suit, then his effect now was positively nuclear. She had a fuzzy memory of the last time they'd gotten in the spa together, the pleasing amount of bare skin, but the memory had been too hazy to compete with the reality.

And the reality was she was nearly ready to jump out of her own skin, while Brad looked completely unaffected. No doubt he was used to doing this sort of thing on a regular basis. Elegant restaurants, beautiful women, hot tubs. She, on the other hand, felt like a fish in the wrong tub of water.

Brad eased down beside her and it took all of her effort not to glide across to the other side and keep him at a distance. Maybe bubbling water and naked skin didn't bother him, but she was positively rabid.

Nervously Kara reached behind her to play with the row of switches on the wall, needing to do something with her hands. Anything to delay having to look at Brad. "I wonder what these are for." She experimented. The first one brought the soft sounds of music. Desperately smiling too brightly at Brad, she tried the next one, which dimmed the lights, casting a nighttime magic to their interlude.

She immediately reached for the switch to turn them off, needing to remove the romantic atmosphere, but Brad caught her hand. "Leave it."

"It kind of reminds me of home," she admitted breathlessly, feeling his hand continue to hold hers. Ripples of sensation danced up from his hand to tantalize the skin of her arm and radiate beyond. Nervously she swallowed.

Brad intended to release her hand.

He certainly never intended to run his fingers up her arm. Nor to massage the tender skin of her neck, then travel toward the shadowed flesh of her delicate collarbone. But once there, he couldn't resist kissing that spot. Feeling her trembling response, he grew bolder.

Perhaps he'd misjudged her feelings. Maybe there *was* a shred of attraction there. He wouldn't find out if he stopped now. Nuzzling her neck, he tasted the sweet scent that always intrigued him. Violets and musk—an intoxicating cross between innocence and allure.

Cupping her chin, he felt the smooth softness of her skin. But once he was that close, he couldn't resist slanting his lips across hers. A remembered sensation of kissing her before roared up like a runaway train. One that threatened to derail him if he wasn't careful.

But it wasn't a night to be careful.

When her lips opened to accept the searching quest of his tongue, he pulled her even closer, reaching up to slip down the straps of her bathing suit. She didn't protest and her breasts, firm and full, spilled into his hands.

She was as lovely as he'd imagined.

His hands roamed over the rounded flesh, before he dipped to taste her pouting nipples. Hearing her moan nearly unleashed the last of his control. He pulled her close, abrading her nipples with the brush of his chest while he reclaimed her lips. Their legs tangled together, sealing the heat.

He angled his head back, nibbling on her neck as he reached to pull down her suit. "No candles and champagne this time, but..."

Brad felt her body go rigid. Meeting her gaze, he saw the light dawn in her eyes and instantly realized his mistake. Praying he was wrong, that she hadn't remembered, he moved to reclaim her lips, but they were unresponsive. Drawing back, he met her eyes—and saw the wrath there.

He gulped, wishing he'd kept his big mouth shut.

"You!" She was practically spitting fire. "You stole my clothes, turned off the electricity in the house and got me drunk!"

"Not exactly—"

"Don't give me that!"

"I didn't plan on getting you drunk. You did that all by yourself!"

"But what *did* you have planned?"

"Not that much," he hedged, realizing he was sinking and for a moment thinking it might be preferable to the battle he saw coming.

"So you did plan the whole thing!"

"I thought if we knew each other better, maybe we'd get along—"

"Better?" she questioned with uncontained anger.

"Get the whole sex thing over with, so it wasn't getting in the way of our... relationship," he reasoned, realizing that as he spoke it was only getting worse.

"Get it over with?" Her body, face and voice were now all rigid—with fury. "And is that what tonight was about, too? The restaurant, the supposedly unavailable suite, the black silk dress you slipped in my bag? So that you could get on with things, so to speak?"

"I didn't have anything to do with your dress. And you're making it sound—"

"I'm making it sound? This from a man who considers making love, 'getting it over with'?"

"I thought it would ease some of the tension between us, from sleeping in the same bed, pretending—"

Grasping the side of the tub, she pulled herself out, shaking off the water as she stalked over to retrieve a towel. "Not to worry." She gestured toward the chaise lounge. "At least here you won't be forced into sharing a bed with me, because you can sleep there!"

"Does that mean the charade for your mother's over, too?"

Hurt flickered across her face and he felt an instant stab of remorse. He hadn't intended to hurt her. But Kara didn't reply. Slamming the bathroom door behind her, she left an ominous silence. One Brad suspected would be a long time in healing.

BRAD WOULD HAVE DESCRIBED Kara's mood the following days as a winter freeze, but Houston's warm to hot temperatures didn't allow such a comparison.

After a stormy evening, a long cold day at the auction, an equally frigid plane ride, they'd returned home in a tense, uncomfortable silence. What made it worse was he could remember the feel of her in his hands, the taste of her on his lips.

And both were driving him crazy.

She on the other hand looked entirely cool and collected. Except when they'd faced her mother for the first time after their return. Then she'd tensed, as though expecting him to be a complete cad and confess everything to Muriel. Instead he'd handled all the luggage, winking at Muriel as he'd elaborated on his time away with Kara, making it sound like a delightful newlywed getaway.

Kara had abandoned her stony expression only long enough for relief to flash across her face. Then she'd returned to old granite face. And anytime they got near the hot tub, she flashed him a look that would have withered lesser men.

"Looks like you've got the weight of the world on your shoulders, son."

Whirling around, Brad stared in surprise at Erastus. "I didn't hear you come up."

Erastus shrugged. "It's an old man's trick. Sometimes it helps to have the element of surprise."

"I used to think so."

"Didn't the trip to Fort Worth go well?"

Brad stared at him quizzically. "Did we tell you about that?"

Erastus waved a hand. "Nope. But you got plenty of people around here to ask."

Thinking he meant Muriel, Brad nodded in agreement. "Auction was all right. Got rid of the second wrong set of pairs. Got some more proven layers."

"Glad to hear it. But that's not what I meant. You're mooning around like a lovesick pup. 'Spect you and the missus had a disagreement."

That was an understatement. Resenting the roles they were forced to play and feeling as though he were onstage, Brad managed a smile. "Nothing serious. You know how women are."

But Erastus didn't return his smile. "That I do." Gazing out over the lay of the land, he finally turned his farseeing gaze back to Brad. "Women like to be treated special. Even if they're saying they don't."

Brad started to dismiss the words, but they stuck in his brain. Maybe the old guy was right. Brad had certainly never intended to blurt out what he had to Kara. *Get it over with.*

Now what woman wouldn't be bowled over with those romantic words? He'd already called himself a fool a thousand times over. Especially when he really wanted to tell her what a very special woman she was—one who had wormed herself under his skin. One he thought of constantly—in and out of bed.

But now he'd blown it. She'd probably had more sophisticated advances from gawky adolescents when she was a teenager.

Special. That's what Erastus had said. And he had a sixty-year marriage to base his advice on.

Brad shoved back his hat. "You know, Erastus. You've got a funny way of showing up at just the right times."

"Do say. Well, what do you know about that? My Sarah always said the same thing."

"Then she was a wise woman." Brad hesitated, then considered the older man's obvious experience. "What did you do to treat Sarah special?"

"Oh, nothing big. It's the little things they like. Mostly knowing that you're thinking about 'em all the time. That you take their interests to heart, putting them above your own."

As though a moment had gone by that he hadn't thought about Kara. But she was different from the other women he'd known. He'd never needed someone else's advice about how to handle the women he'd dated in the past, but Kara remained a mystery. One who wouldn't be swayed by expensive trinkets and weekend flings in exotic ports. While she'd made it plain she was into this marriage for the ranch only, still she clung to old-fashioned values. Ones that made him think of picket fences and a woman who wanted to be courted.

That, too, was an outdated notion. But somehow it applied to Kara. He still winced at the memory of his words to Kara that night in the hotel. Nothing had come out as he'd intended and she didn't look as though she were willing to give him a second chance.

Meeting Erastus's wise gaze, Brad knew he had to try. Realizing he hadn't asked the older man for a word of advice about the ostriches, Brad wondered suddenly just when Kara had become more important to him than the ranch.

"DON'T FORGET TO PROTECT your feet, too." Stopping at the entrance to the nursery housing the new-born chicks, Kara handed her mother plastic covers for her boots. "If we spread bacteria into the nursery, it could wipe out the entire flock."

Muriel fitted the covers over her boots and then they opened the door to the expected blast of steamy heat. It was an exact process, requiring a steady beginning temperature of ninety-five degrees and controlled humidity. It definitely catered to bird rather than human comfort.

"Oh, aren't they cute?" Muriel cooed as the plump, fuzzy chicks came into sight. Downy, light brown with distinctive spots, the animated Brillo pads were charmers.

"A lot of trouble though," Kara sighed, inwardly agreeing with Brad though she'd never admit it. "Even though it only takes a month and a half for the eggs to hatch, then you have to be so careful about disease, feeding, even getting them to drink the water."

"I think I heard this from Brad, but as I recall you were defending the tiny terrors."

Kara shrugged. "Who'd have thought we would lose chicks because that seemingly shallow water bowl was too deep and they drowned? And that if they huddled together they'd smother each other?"

Muriel gazed at her daughter. "So you're beginning to agree with Brad."

Kara muttered something unintelligible as she floated tender clover leaves in the water. Loving the taste, the chicks started eating the clover and drinking the water it was in.

"Clever trick," Muriel commented. "But then you've always been a smart girl."

"Most of the time."

"I can't help but notice that you and Brad haven't exactly been cozy lately."

Dismay struck Kara as she glanced up sharply at her mother. The one thing she didn't want to do was tip her off to the situation. But the hurt Kara had been feeling since the disastrous night in the hotel had been hard to contain. She'd used a wall of anger to insulate herself against Brad, but apparently Muriel had seen through that wall. Kara longed to unburden herself to her mother as she'd done so often in the past. Regrettably she'd set up a situation that made that impossible.

"You know how it is, Mom. Two people adjusting to each other."

"That might be easier without a third wheel always around."

"It's not you," Kara argued truthfully. It was the two of them. Especially since she'd mistakenly believed that Brad had actually begun to feel something, at least to be as attracted to her as she was to him. But to him it was merely a physical urge. An itch he could scratch without any messy emotional complications. And for some inexplicable reason, that hurt terribly.

"I could get a short lease on an apartment," Muriel offered.

"And pay the mortgage note on your house at the same time?" Kara shook her head. "You're not going to put yourself in debt when we have this huge house. No, there's plenty of room for three people." *Unless two of them included Kara and Brad.*

"I'm not sure—"

"You're hardly ever around, Mom. You and Chuck are always going someplace."

Muriel glanced down at the chicks running pell-mell between the barriers. "He's acting different lately. I didn't see him at all while you were on your trip."

"Maybe he's had a lot of flights."

"That's what he says. But I don't know..." Her voice trailed off as her face grew pensive.

"It's not like you two are serious."

Muriel couldn't quite hide the shaft of pain that filled her expression. "I guess not."

Kara studied her mother, awareness hitting like an unwanted thunderbolt. "You care for him, don't you?"

Nodding, Muriel managed a strained smile. "But I've been out of this dating game thing for a long time. I guess I misread how he was feeling."

Appalled, Kara could only bite back the comments struggling to get free. Wondering suddenly what Brad had told Chuck, Kara knew they had to undo what they'd done. Caught up in her own mixed feelings about Brad, she hadn't stopped to really consider what Chuck meant to her mother. Or the hurt Muriel was apparently feeling. "I don't think so, Mom."

"Or maybe he's just tired of me. I'm sure he could find someone younger, prettier."

Kara could have groaned aloud. They'd apparently managed to sabotage something very special. Feeling incredibly selfish, Kara could only pat her mother's shoulder, knowing that she had to confront Brad so they could fix this mess. And suddenly that sounded about as appealing as another dip in the hot tub.

Chapter Nine

Nervously Kara rehung Aunt Tillie's portrait in the
living room and then, knowing she couldn't postpone
the inevitable any longer, sought out Brad. She'd
waited two days, trying to shore up her courage, but
she needed to face the problem they'd created. The
situation wasn't fair to her mother or Chuck. Not
finding Brad in the house, she walked outside, past the
pool area and toward the stables.

He was standing beside the corral, a tall silhouette
against the encroaching darkness. His Stetson was
tilted back on his head as he studied the empty circle
where horses once stamped impatiently to be free, to
be ridden on the then unfettered range.

Appreciating the pure male beauty of his stance, the
ebony hair that spilled beneath the brim of his hat, the
strong lines of a face she knew as well as her own,
Kara held her silence.

Not wanting to disturb the moment, she glanced at
his blunt, strong hands that gripped the railing, and
remembered his touch, feeling the responding heat
rush to fill her. Because even as she'd ended that moment in the hotel, she'd wanted desperately for it to

continue, to know the fulfillment his eyes had promised.

He turned, apparently having heard her despite her stillness. His eyes lit for a moment, then shuttered as he turned back to the unoccupied corral.

"It needs horses," she offered as she joined him at the rail.

He was quiet for a moment and she wondered if he intended to turn the tables, awarding her the same silent treatment she'd been giving him. "Been a long time since this ranch needed horses."

She studied the emptiness of the corral, its bleak loneliness. "Need's a funny thing. Maybe just wanting them ought to be enough."

Brad angled his head toward her, intently studying her face as though trying to determine if there was a hidden meaning to her words. "Maybe."

She took a deep breath and plowed on. "I talked to my mother today. Chuck hasn't been to see her since you talked to him. I know it was partly my idea, but I think it was a bad one. Apparently... she really cares for him. It may be inconvenient for us, but—"

"I've already talked to Chuck. Today, at the airport. Told him that we just wanted to make sure he didn't blow our cover and to forget everything I'd told him."

"What?"

"After I talked with Chuck I realized that he really cared for Muriel. Before that, I thought she was just another notch on his belt loop. But she's... different." An unreadable expression crossed his face, then disappeared.

Kara held her temper in check with an effort, her earlier goodwill dissipating. "You did all this without consulting me?"

Exasperated, he turned to her. "You just told me how Muriel feels."

"But you acted before I told you—"

"I figured we'd butted into her life and Chuck's because we were only thinking about ourselves. Seemed a tad selfish, don't you think?"

More than a tad. But she hated to admit that. She also hated to admit that Brad had been more sensitive to the situation than she had. Then an even more overwhelming emotion hit her.

Respect.

For the man who'd discarded his own interests because he recognized that Muriel and Chuck's relationship was in jeopardy.

Grateful that he was that kind of person, she gathered her composure. "You're right."

He blinked, then stared at her. "I'm sorry. My hearing must be going."

Kara gripped the railing beneath her fingers, ignoring the tiny splinter that dug beneath her skin. "I said—you're right. And I'm glad you were thoughtful enough to straighten things out before they were hopelessly ruined. My mother cares a great deal for Chuck and I think their relationship should have a chance. Two people who are so drawn to each other shouldn't be kept apart."

Brad's gaze caught and held hers. The moment stretched out as Kara's mouth dried and her throat developed an impossible lump.

His hand reached out to cover hers, caressing each knuckle, then turning her hand upside down to fold within his own. The movement drove the splinter in deeper and she flinched involuntarily.

"What is it?"

She pointed to the hand he held. "Splinter."

The strain on his face eased into a roguish smile. "That falls within my line of expertise."

"Oh?" She held her breath as he released her hand to hold only her finger, and then pulled that finger into the dim light of the carriage lantern hanging on the gate. Automatically she moved closer, as well.

Her breath quickened as she realized they were scarcely inches apart. Reaching into his pocket, he removed a knife.

She gulped. "You aren't intending to cut it out with that, are you?"

He chuckled. "Nope. It's a Swiss army knife with a few attachments." Unfolding it, he quickly pulled out the splinter with one of the implements before she could protest.

"Ouch!"

His voice was dry. "I think you'll live." Yet he lifted her finger to his lips and sucked the offended spot.

A thrill ricocheted through her with jet-propelled speed. Images of those lips doing that same thing where his hands had once rested made her nipples pucker at the thought. Glad of the concealing darkness, she instantly regretted her choice of a thin T-shirt.

Her voice was brittle with forced laughter as she retrieved her finger. "I'm okay."

"I didn't think it was terminal." The wry tone was lost in the deep huskiness of his voice.

She jammed her hands into her pockets, incredibly nervous. Even more aware of him. The silence that stretched between them unnerved her. "Have you been riding long?" she blurted.

"Excuse me?"

"Horses," she explained, wishing she possessed a little more smooth sophistication. Every time she opened her mouth, she sounded like a dolt. She had an image of the type of woman he was no doubt used to. Somehow she doubted she'd fill that mold.

The evening breeze trickled through the giant magnolia tree that grew nearby, sending a luscious wave of scent over the dew-soaked grass. Senses heightened, Kara could also smell the clean scent that was uniquely Brad's. Having slept next to him, she realized she could pick him out of a hundred men, even if she was blindfolded. It was an intriguing thought.

"Do you really want to talk about horses?" he asked softly, reaching out at the same time to capture a wayward strand of hair that the breeze lifted.

Her scalp tingled beneath the touch, and she could feel his heat. Weakness made its way through her body. "Um...yes. I don't know that much about you," she answered, stalling even as the air seemed to grow thicker, tighter.

His hands moved from her hair to caress the back of her neck. "I've loved horses since I was a kid. Started riding when I was about eight. Found this place a few years later and I've wanted it ever since." His fingers slid around her shoulders and then down her arms, moving back up again to rest beneath her chin, then to shadow the hollows of her throat. "Is that what you wanted to know?"

"Um." Her answer came out as a strangled sound when he angled his head so that his breath teased her cheek, his lips resting just beyond the reach of her own.

"And I used to believe there was nothing as beautiful as this ranch," he continued before dropping his lips to the corner of her mouth, nibbling that tender flesh.

The words barely registered as she opened her mouth to receive his kiss. He wasn't abrupt; instead he savored the moment as though each taste were a drink of fine wine. And she was drowning in the heady bouquet he provided. Shudders rushed through her as if on a race to a predetermined finish line.

His hands traveled down her back, then traced a line up her rib cage, igniting a path of pure desire. Restraining the moan that threatened to erupt, she leaned into him.

"There you are!" Muriel's excited voice penetrated Kara's consciousness.

Mortified, Kara drew back. *This was for show?* She'd thought he'd been attracted. More, she'd thought he was beginning to have some feeling for her. Stung, she could barely rest in the easy embrace he kept around her waist, wishing instead that she could jerk away and slink into the cover of darkness. He must think she was a fool, ready to fall into his arms with the slightest persuasion. Determinedly she stared ahead, feeling the heat of two red spots she was certain dotted her cheeks.

"We were just going in swimming," Muriel added, a glow of pleasure lighting her face. "Won't you join us?"

Although Kara was delighted to see Chuck and her mother together again, all she wanted to do was escape. "I don't think so—" She stopped when she felt a slight but distinctive pinch from Brad, who made it appear that he was merely deepening his embrace.

"You two want to be alone?" Chuck asked pointedly, his ever-present grin back in force.

Maybe they'd acted too quickly in rejoining these two. Chuck was enjoying himself. Too much.

"I thought we could grill some hamburgers," Muriel added.

"Add some heat to the night," Chuck volunteered, his action underlining his words as his arm looped around Muriel's shoulders.

"We'll be glad to join you," Brad answered. "Just give us time to change."

After Muriel and Chuck left for the pool, Kara turned on Brad. "Why did you agree to join them?"

"Both of them are walking on air right now. Your mother looks like a kid on Christmas Day. You want to spoil that?"

She could cheerfully choke him. First for abrading her emotions, then for being so cussedly right.

"I'll go swimming," she agreed, unable to hide her pout. "But this is just for *show*."

He looked momentarily affronted, then remembered Erastus's advice and grinned at her. "Of course. What else?"

WHAT ELSE? THE WORDS jangled around in her brain like a broken record of someone running his fingernails down a blackboard. Mostly because now she had to spend an evening watching Brad cavort in those damned swimming trunks that made her lascivious thoughts run wild. Or maybe because she had to confront the truth—that she'd imagined what she thought was growing between them.

It was the second thought that kept her quiet most of the evening, even though the others laughed and joked with ease. Brad certainly seemed unaffected by what had passed between them. The kiss was apparently forgotten. He must have ice water in his veins.

Muriel smiled at Brad just then, before linking arms with Chuck. Not ice water, Kara amended unhappily. Otherwise he wouldn't have repaired the damage they'd nearly caused between her mother and Chuck. Brad simply seemed to be immune to her own charms.

Kara glanced down at the modest cover-up she still wore. For a moment she imagined changing into a daring bikini, then whipping off the cover-up to torment Brad. But the idea faded as fast as it formed.

She was chicken.

Not about anything else. She'd challenge Brad on almost every count. But she wasn't going to act like a ridiculous femme fatale, especially when she couldn't seem to heat Brad's temperature beyond a basic physical urge that she expected could be accomplished if he was comatose.

"Aren't you coming in?" Chuck called to her from the pool. The three of them glided around in the water that was lit by the bright lights suspended from the surrounding trees. They all looked far happier than she felt.

Shrugging, Kara removed the terry cover-up, revealing the flattering one-piece suit that showcased her legs, then dove cleanly into the water. She surfaced, seeing Chuck and Muriel swimming side by side ahead of her. Pivoting, she didn't see Brad. Not sure whether to be relieved or annoyed, she kicked her feet out and floated on her back. Determined to relax and avoid him, she dangled her arms in the water, moving them languidly, just enough to keep afloat.

Surreptitiously glancing around, she still couldn't see any sign of Brad. Ridiculous disappointment surfaced. *Fine, now I'm wishing he was around to torment me.*

But the thought disappeared as she felt a sudden yank from beneath. Dunking beneath the water, she flailed out but couldn't surface immediately. Then those same familiar arms reached around her and yanked her to the surface.

Gasping, she spit out a mouthful of water as she glared at Brad. "Why'd you do that?"

His expression was absurdly innocent. "I had to get your attention."

Skimming her hand across the water, she splashed as much as possible in his face.

But he only laughed, shaking the water easily from his dark mane of hair. Then he slicked his hands back over the unruly locks. Kara watched the play of muscles in his forearms and biceps that accompanied the movement.

"We have to practice if we're going to beat Chuck and your mother at volleyball. And don't even think about ducking out. They're already wondering why you're acting so standoffish."

As though he couldn't guess. Still she couldn't repress a groan. She wanted to do her part to repair the damage to Chuck and Muriel's relationship, and she'd hardly been cooperative so far. Brad was right. Her behavior had been poor. Once again she'd been thinking only of herself. Looking over Brad's shoulder, she could see her mother perched on Chuck's shoulders, laughing as he twirled her around the pool.

This was worse than double-dating with a couple of hormonal teenagers. Kara could just imagine sitting on Brad's shoulders in that same far too intimate position.

But he didn't give her time to think about it. Instead he reached around her and pulled her up on his shoulders in one quick movement so that she sat above water level, enabling her to play volleyball.

Kara's thighs trembled as they rested against his chest. But they competed for weakness with her calves since Brad held them loosely in his hands to keep her balanced.

"We're going to beat the..." Chuck began, then laughed as he apparently tickled Muriel, who hooted at the action. "I guess it couldn't be *socks* we'd beat off you." He measured them with a long, probing glance. "But we could play for something more interesting."

"Like what?" Brad challenged.

Kara restrained from kicking him. Barely.

"Dinner at Maxim's," Chuck responded. "And a night of dancing."

"You're on," Brad replied.

Kara settled for yanking a lock of his hair instead.

But his hands moved up to clamp around her knees. A ball hit the air. And the battle was on.

Water splashed and flew out onto the patio as though they were trying to empty the pool. Getting into the spirit of the game, Kara forgot they were supposed to lose.

"Wimps!" Brad yelled as Chuck nearly unseated Muriel while moving her out of the path of a fast, incoming shot.

"Just because you newlyweds are welded together doesn't mean we all are!" Chuck shouted back, a knowing, mischievous grin splitting his face.

"When I get my hands on him, he'll be lucky if all I do is drown him," Brad muttered.

Kara could feel the fire heating her face as her mother laughed appreciatively before tossing the ball back across the water.

"Kara's always been an affectionate person," Muriel chimed in. "Right, Brad?"

Feeling his hands clench convulsively around her knees, Kara spared Brad a moment of pity before she served the ball as hard as possible—a fast-moving blur of white that sped at their opponents. Seeing their simultaneous expressions of surprise was worth it.

As Chuck and Muriel scrambled to return the ball, Kara leaned forward, trying to forget their words. Despite the rapidly moving game, she couldn't forget the heated feeling of being so close to Brad. With each return and volley she was aware of him moving beneath her, his hands holding her close.

Imagining how it would feel to remain near, she didn't see the fast-moving return that lobbed across the pool.

The ball bounced away and they lost.

Chuck and Muriel shrieked with delight as he lifted her from his shoulders and then kissed her soundly. Brad didn't move for a moment, then ducked beneath the water so Kara could slide off. Self-consciously they stared at the other couple, the rippling water in the pool, at anything but each other.

When Chuck finally approached, Brad made his voice hearty. "Congratulations. You'll have a great night out."

"Oh, we're not going alone," Chuck replied, a smirk illuminating his handsome face.

"What do you mean?" Kara asked as she stared at the smiling pair.

"You're going with us. I specified a night out—not for how many people," Chuck answered smoothly.

A romantic night on the town, including dancing. Kara swallowed her sigh. And did the only thing she could think of. She sank beneath the concealing water, leaving only a ripple.

THE RESTAURANT WAS exquisite, the food delicious, the service flawless. But Brad felt as though the stiffly starched collar of his white dress shirt would choke him. And his silk tie had an equal stranglehold on him. Because sitting only inches from him, Kara's bare shoulders gleamed in the dim lighting and the scent of her unusual perfume stole through his senses.

Slow torture, concocted by his friend to repay him for nearly derailing his relationship with Muriel. Brad supposed it was a fair punishment, but at the moment he wasn't sure he'd be able to endure it.

And for some reason Kara seemed nervous. And that was something he'd only seen in her once—the first time her mother had come for dinner. Angry, obstinate, and foolishly impulsive, yes. But not nervous. Maybe she, too, wished she was anywhere else. It was too reminiscent of their night in Dallas.

She'd certainly kicked and balked enough about coming. By early afternoon she had invented so many ludicrous excuses that he fully expected her to develop a terminal hangnail. However he hadn't expected her to dress so sensuously.

Provocative in jeans and a T-shirt, she was downright deadly in flowing silk. Seeing admiring glances
from nearby male diners, Brad wished for the hun-
dredth time that Kara had chosen something more sedate. Something that didn't reveal quite so much skin.

Logic told him that it was a perfectly respectable
dinner dress, one that dipped low in the front, even
lower in the back. But some sort of unexplainable acid
was eating away at his gut, demanding that he retrieve her cloak and wrap her in it. He must be going
crazy. In the past he'd enjoyed the envious glances
other men had given the beautiful women he escorted. Those looks had never made him want to
knock down the offenders and rip the woman away
from her admirers.

Kara angled her face back, meeting his brooding
glance. She offered him a tentative glance. "Do I have
lipstick on my nose or something?"

It was something, all right. "No. Everything's just
where it's supposed to be." Which was driving him
crazy.

"I think my mother and Chuck have patched things
up nicely."

"That's something I've had second thoughts
about."

One eyebrow barely lifted. "Oh?"

He shook his head, not concentrating on the other
couple as his gaze never left Kara. "Chuck's enjoying
this too much. I have a feeling he's going to put us in
the hot seat the first chance he gets."

Kara glanced down at the immaculate white linen
tablecloth, then played her fingers nervously over the
stem of her wineglass. "Maybe he's already started."

Their eyes met for a charged moment. The music, along with the clink of cutlery against china, faded. A waiter approached the table, sized them up and wisely changed course.

Brad watched the golden flecks swim in those incredible green eyes before they turned smoky and dark. He'd come to recognize all the nuances of her expressions. The arch look that accompanied anger or mutiny. The softening that started as her mouth dropped open slightly, her lips full and waiting, her eyes languidly expectant.

Kara watched as his hands slipped over her arm, caressing the soft skin between her wrist and elbow. Liquid heat exploded and she felt a damp response center between her thighs as he continued the exquisite assault. He traced a line up her bare shoulder, then to the needy flesh of her neck. By the time he angled his head toward hers, she wanted to beg for the kiss. Instead she looked around for her mother, to see if this was a calculated move.

Muriel was nowhere in sight.

Something between a sigh and a groan emerged. Then his lips were on hers, and she opened herself to the kiss. His exploration made her want to climb from her own chair to wrap herself around him. It was madness. She knew he didn't care for her, but at the moment that didn't seem important. What was important was the longing he made her feel. One that was wrapped up in sensation and emotion.

The string quartet ended the lively waltz and turned to a quieter, more evocative tune. And Kara concentrated on listening to the music rather than the logic that marched relentlessly through her mind.

Pulling away from Brad, trying to act composed, she watched her mother and Chuck dancing. It was as though now that they were back together, neither wanted to be parted.

The beeper at Brad's waist chirped. He looked ready to throw it through the nearest window, so Kara released his arm. "I think you'd better hear the message first, *then* turn the beeper into sawdust."

Reluctantly he agreed and headed for the pay phone.

Returning to the table, he looked at three expectant pairs of eyes, since Muriel and Chuck had rejoined Kara. "Four pilots down. Part of the hangar damaged in the last storm collapsed. They were inside playing poker." He cursed softly, then shoved a hand through his hair. "I hate this, but I've got to get out there. If we don't make these flights I'll lose some of my best contracts."

"That means me, too," Chuck said to Muriel.

"Of course you have to go," she answered calmly.

Brad's gaze zeroed in on Kara, his eyes conveying his regret. "It sounds like an all-nighter. We'll call if that changes."

Kara smiled weakly, feeling the pins being knocked from under her. Because at the rate they'd been progressing, she'd expected a far different outcome for the evening.

Muriel and Kara watched the men leave, both tall and handsome, cutting a swath as they wound through the restaurant.

Kara looked at her mother, expecting a sage, philosophical word of comfort.

In some ways, Muriel didn't disappoint her. "Rats."

Chapter Ten

It had been a long, exhausting night. Brad glanced over at Chuck, seeing the matching weariness on his friend's face. Brad twisted the steering wheel of his four-by-four as they pulled into the ranch, immeasurably glad finally to be home. They'd had to double up on flights. Luckily he'd rounded up two standby pilots early in the morning.

But he and Chuck were facing a lot of flights until his regular crew recuperated. Only one injury was serious, but a combination of broken bones, one wrenched shoulder, and a concussion would keep them grounded until they healed up enough to resume flying.

Right now regret overrode fatigue as he thought of the aborted ending to the previous evening. Because for once he hadn't blown it with Kara. And the night might have meant lasting changes for them. Brad didn't want to examine just how deep that meaning went, but he accepted that things were moving in a new direction.

"What's that?" Chuck asked as they came to a stop. He pointed to a large van that was pulling away from the ranch and toward the road.

"We sold some of the younger birds to a meat packer," Brad explained as they climbed out of the vehicle.

Chuck made a face of distaste.

"Don't knock it. A few restaurants in big cities are serving ostrich meat."

"Where? Outer Mongolia?"

Brad thought for a minute. "Dallas. And at some of the best restaurants."

Chuck looked skeptical. "Name one."

"Huntington's in the Westin Hotel. They serve ostrich steak with sun-dried blueberry chutney."

"Yuck."

"They make a mean ostrich chili."

He shrugged. "That might be okay, but give me cholesterol-filled, fatty beef any day."

"But you know ostrich is lean, low-fat, low-cholesterol—"

"Save it for the customers. I want my burgers dripping with grease, not nutrition."

Brad laughed, not taking offense. "At thirty dollars a pound, I don't imagine McDonald's will be selling ostrich burgers anytime soon."

Chuck scratched at the stubble on his chin. "Thirty bucks a pound? Hey, you guys taking in any investors?"

"I thought you wanted grease—"

"I don't have to eat 'em to know that's a lot of money. Birdie by the pound. Catchy, huh?"

"Not quite," Kara answered from the porch.

Both men looked up.

"Morning," Brad greeted her, some of his weariness slipping away as he drank in the sight of her leaning against one of the columns, smooth golden hair tossed over one shoulder, a formfitting T-shirt and jeans hugging those curves he'd thought about all night.

He waited for her answer.

And didn't get one.

He finally noticed what his fatigue-dampened senses hadn't picked up on before. She was mad. Hopping mad.

"What's under your skin?" he asked, wondering what he'd done to anger her, especially considering he hadn't been around all night.

"Does B & W Meat Packers ring a bell?" she asked evenly.

"Sure, the van that just left. Did the driver get all the birds they bought? I listed the ID numbers on the bill of sale."

"How convenient." She tucked her chin in like a boxer. "And when were you planning on telling me about this little sale?"

Exhaustion allowed a bit of his own temper to emerge. It was one thing to work all night. It was another to come home from that job to an angry, unreasonable woman. "Oh, about the same time the little old mortgage note was paid," he replied tersely, mocking her Southern style of speech.

"And I was just supposed to agree to let our birds be turned into the Colonel's biggest batch of southern-fried in the hemisphere?" Her voice rose as she spoke, ending on a near shriek.

He kept his voice purposely low. "I don't recall asking for your consensus."

She sucked in a fortifying breath. "So you admit you sold our birds without even consulting me? Expecting me to go along with your idea of murdering them?"

"*Murder?* Don't get so dramatic. They're birds, stock. Nothing more. The idea of selling the eggs and feathers when we can get contracts for them is fine. But we need money right now. I'm not letting your sentimentality ruin a perfectly good business deal."

"I'm not letting those birds get slaughtered," she countered.

"I don't need your permission."

"And I don't need your *orders,*" she retorted. "I quit the best job of my life because I couldn't stand to take orders and I won't start taking them from you."

"This time you will," he replied, anger and fatigue outweighing reason. "In case you haven't noticed, I've been draining the profits from the air charter business to float this place."

"Airplanes are things. The ostriches are living beings!"

Brad felt his pride take a hit and along with it a good dose of hurt at her continued dismissal of his life's work. "As usual you've summed up my business as being meaningless. Holbrook Enterprises may not be important to you, but it is to me and it's time you learned that." A flicker of pain crossed his face. He'd thought she was the one person who knew how much the business meant to him. Certainly far more than just a pile of machinery. It was tied up in who he was—and the memory of his brother. Apparently she hadn't cared to remember that. Purposely he hardened his voice. "I'm not going to endanger my business any longer. This month's mortgage note is coming from the sale of the birds. Period."

"I don't think so," she replied in a tone that was too cool for comfort.

"And what are you going to do about it?"

"This." Calmly she opened her hand and let a pile of shredded paper fall to the ground.

One piece caught his eye and Brad picked it up, reading enough to make him see red. "This is the contract with B & W."

"Precisely. I told them we wouldn't be needing their services in the future."

"Don't be so sure," he replied, his voice low, infuriated. "I might be selling them fillet of bird lady if you don't tell me this is a mistake."

"No mistake." She angled her head toward the far pens. "The birds are still here and the contract with B & W is history. We can wait for a zoo contract, but we're not selling them to a packing house!" After opening the screen door, she stepped inside and slammed it behind her.

Brad cursed loudly and vehemently.

Chuck waited patiently, then let out a low whistle. "Love is bliss, son."

"For two cents I'd leave right now," Brad raged. "It's a damn good thing this marriage isn't real, because Kara's the last woman on earth I'd marry! Willful, obstinate. Thinks more of those damn birds than a business I built with nothing more than my two hands!"

"And a nice little Cessna 421," Chuck inserted calmly. "What say we go have a cool one, bid the ladies goodbye and then crash?"

"You bid the ladies anything you want. I'm out of here."

"Hey, man—" Chuck protested.

"You're flying days, I'm taking evenings." Brad glared in the direction of the front door. "At least I'll be spared spending the nights here." Not waiting for an answer, he spun around, marched to his Land Rover, then roared away.

KARA NURSED HER BRUISED feelings as she examined the sagging wire of the newest pens she'd built. Brad's angry words replayed themselves in her head, as they had for the past week.

It's a damn good thing this marriage isn't real, because Kara's the last woman on earth I'd marry!

Involuntarily she flinched, still unbearably stung by his words. They were more than cruel, because they were a direct hit on the truth. Brad would never have married her on his own and his feelings in that regard apparently hadn't changed. An intimate setting like Maxim's had momentarily obscured that reality. A romantic evening didn't change what they had. Still, she'd hoped, wanted . . .

Yet after Brad had exhibited his need to be in control, she wasn't sure she wanted their relationship to change. Control was the one thing she couldn't tolerate. Logically she realized it was tied up with her mother's lack of control for many years, emotionally she simply couldn't bear the thought of someone issuing orders. And, with a painful lump of truth, she also knew she didn't want a loveless marriage. Her parents' union had taught her that. Still she felt overwhelmed by a haunting disappointment.

Glancing up, Kara focused on the broken-down ostrich pens. Resembling pretzels, the wire stuck up every which way from the constant pecking by the ostriches. As she watched in dismay, one of the females unrepentantly snatched at one of the few remaining upright rows of screening.

Whipping off her baseball hat, Kara ran toward the bird, shooing her away. "Look what you did," she scolded, trying without success to prop the misshapen fencing back into place.

"I told you that wire wasn't heavy enough."

Kara stiffened immediately, not certain she wanted to turn and face Brad. He'd made it clear he didn't want to see her. True he'd been flying all night, every night, which prevented him from coming home. But she was sure he could have made some time to be at the ranch. Chuck certainly had. As though afraid a repeat performance would occur, Chuck had been as attentive as possible to Muriel, spending every evening with her.

Kara faced the solitary nights, not sure if and when the situation would change. Brad had turned uncommunicative and closed. And she'd die before she'd admit how lonely her bed felt.

While she had spent many nights deliberately holding herself stiffly aloof rather than roll toward the inviting embrace of his arms, still she'd grown used to the weight of him next to her, anchoring the mattress in place. She missed the indentation his head made in the pillow, the warm solidness of his body just an outstretched arm away. The way he lit a room with just his grin.

Now he seemed miles away.

Since the episode with B & W Meat Packers, Brad had slept at the hangar in his office, using his work as an excuse not to return home. She'd been shocked that he'd virtually turned over the running of the ranch to her. His anger was great enough that he didn't even call to see if he was needed at the helm.

Resorting to leaving messages with his secretary or notes for Brad to find explaining what was going on at the ranch, Kara had struggled to keep the operation on an even keel. The amount of book work was staggering and she was surprised that Brad had never mentioned it. She'd certainly given him enough grief about his persnickety ways.

Shadowing her eyes from the sun with an upraised hand, Kara leaned against one of the tilted fence posts, ones she hadn't set in cement as he'd suggested. "I thought you were flying." She didn't think any such thing, knowing he'd taken the night shift to avoid spending the nights with her.

"Two of my guys are back," he answered briefly.

Glancing up at him, she wondered suddenly if he'd come to say goodbye. His expression was so serious and intent. Her heart started beating wildly as a band of pain clutched her.

In a terrifying but clear realization it hit her. She loved him. A man who wanted to control her. A man who didn't love *her*. Despite all his solid, immovable ways. Or perhaps because of them.

This was the culmination of her worst nightmares. She couldn't have filled out a form at a computer dating service and asked for someone more wrong for her. Yet the hitch in her heart told her that she could no more control the emotion than she could fix what stood between them.

She could bow out gracefully. Pack up her things and leave Brad the ranch. Even though she'd grown to love the Rocking J, she now realized that his love of this land had been part of him for far longer. Opening her mouth to make the offer, she was startled by another voice directly behind her.

"Glad to see you back, son. Guess you don't have to fly around the clock anymore." Erastus strolled up to stand between them.

Kara exhaled, not sure whether to bless or curse his interruption.

"I was just telling Kara that two of my pilots are back. We're still shorthanded, but it's manageable."

"Good thing you're here, Brad. I know Kara's missed having you around." Erastus pinned Kara in a wise, brightly blue gaze. "Right?"

Her eyes fled downward, before slowing sliding up to meet Brad's. Reluctantly she nodded her head.

"And you, Brad. All those days and nights away from home..." Erastus shook his head ruefully.

Something indefinable flickered across Brad's face.

"Since you're home now, I'm going to be pushy," Erastus continued. "How 'bout letting me come to dinner tonight? I hate to admit it, but I miss the old place."

Kara scrabbled for excuses. If she was going to bid Brad goodbye, she didn't need an audience.

But Brad surprised her, his voice low and resigned. "Does seven-thirty sound all right? I'll pick up a pizza."

"I'll be here." Erastus's gaze moved beyond them to stare critically at the pens. "But, right now I think we'd better get started on fixing those pens."

"You don't have to—"

"It's not necessary—"

Kara gazed helplessly at Brad. They needed to talk, but she didn't dare open the subject in front of the crafty old man. He'd see the truth and Brad's chance at keeping the ranch would dissolve. With a start, she realized how important it was to her that Brad not lose his dream.

"With an extra set of hands, you can get a lot more accomplished," Erastus insisted.

"I'll need a heavier gauge wire, a few sacks of cement to set the posts in—"

"Not to worry," Erastus interrupted Brad. He pointed to the bed of his pickup truck. "Got it in there. Had it on order at the lumberyard and I'd already paid for it. That's why I came by. To see if you could use it."

"The pen does need to be rebuilt," Kara admitted.

Brad looked at her in surprise but she glanced away, unable to admit he'd been right.

The hours slid by as the three of them worked on the pens, first herding the birds out into the adjacent corral, then tearing out the old posts and wire. Each minute was an agony for Kara as she worked side by side with Brad, unable to talk to him, afraid of what he would say when she did.

Twilight overtook them as they set the last post.

Erastus pushed back his battered hat and wiped at his forehead. "Looks like I'm not going to have time to head home before dinner. Can I wash up here?"

Kara abandoned her musings and collected her manners. "Of course. My mother's going out for the evening. She should be gone by now. Feel free to use the bath next to the study. The repairs on the main bath are taking forever. With all the damage from the storm, every contractor in the area's still behind. Part of the work's finished, but the hall and bath are all still draped in plastic."

"I hate to crowd you young people—"

"You aren't," she interrupted. Purposely avoiding Brad's gaze, she managed a smile for the older man. "We're delighted that you're here."

Shoring up her smile, Kara walked with Erastus toward the front door. When Brad didn't join them, Kara turned back, forcing an even tone in her voice. "You joining us?"

"In a minute."

"Fine." Knowing she sounded overly cheerful, Kara tried to rein in her emotions and behave normally.

Then she glanced back at the birds crowded into the pens. Of course. They needed to be returned to the new area. Even though she didn't want to face Brad, she couldn't let him do all the work.

"I'll be right back, Erastus. I need to help put the birds back."

"I'll wait out on the front porch."

She quickly retraced her steps. Brad's face showed some surprise when she ducked under the fence, but then they quickly started herding the animals. Dust flew and there was a lot of mindless running from one end of the pen to the other, but for the most part the ostriches cooperated.

As the last of the females went through the gate, one of them reached over unexpectedly and snatched the ring suspended on a chain from around Kara's neck.

Her hand darted out to retrieve the ring but she was too late and the bird too fast.

"What was that?" Brad demanded, seeing her battle with the bird.

"My ring," she explained dully, her face stricken.

"Great. Was it big enough to impact the bird?"

She swallowed a lump in her throat, feeling incredibly silly. "I don't think so. It was the ring you bought for me at our...wedding."

Brad stared at her in surprise. "You kept that?"

She looked everywhere but at him. "Yes."

"I didn't see you wearing it."

"It was on a chain around my neck." Kara stared woefully at the innocent-looking bird. "But I guess it's gone forever now."

Startled by the distress he heard in her voice, Brad tried to understand why she'd worn it, or why she cared that it was gone. "It was only a cheap zirconium."

A spurt of pain crossed her features before she closed her expression. "Right...just a zirconium."

"I can't get it back," he explained, feeling he should do more. Not understanding why it mattered to her.

She shrugged. "I know." For a moment she stared at the bird, then back at the ground. "It was pink," she added unnecessarily.

"I remember." He'd felt bad about not providing anything better at the time, but then rationalized that a ring wouldn't mean much in a fake marriage.

"I'd better see about our dinner," she said finally. "Erastus is waiting."

"Right."

He watched as she left, shoulders sagging, returning to the porch to meet up with the older man. If he lived to be a thousand, he'd never understand the strange workings of the female mind. It was not as if she'd lost something of value. He bent to fasten the latch.

Or had she?

As THEY ENTERED THE HOUSE, Erastus smiled at Kara. "I'll make myself at home if you don't mind."

"Of course." It was more his home than theirs, Kara realized. Because he'd filled the house with the love that made it a true home.

As he walked away, she slipped into the dusk-filled living room. For a few minutes, she allowed the darkness to glide over her and wished desperately she could remain in hiding. Instead she sighed and clicked on a small desk lamp. Immediately it illuminated Brad's unusual collection on the side table.

"What are you doing in here all alone?"

Kara whirled around, startled by her mother's voice. "I thought you'd gone out."

"I'm leaving now. I just heard Chuck pulling up outside."

Tamping down her own feelings, Kara smiled. "Have a great time."

"You, too. It's nice for you and Brad to be alone for an evening."

Kara wondered suddenly why her mother hadn't run into Erastus. "But—"

Muriel laughed as she reached out to finger the scarf on the fertility goddess. "I realize Brad's had to work a lot of hours lately, but has this little beauty worked yet?"

Swallowing a strangled reply, Kara was saved from answering as the doorbell rang.

"That'll be Chuck." Muriel leaned forward to kiss Kara's cheek. "Enjoy true love, dear. It only comes once in a lifetime."

With a whirl of perfume, she left. Her voice and laughter quickly chimed with Chuck's. Then the door closed behind them and the truck roared to life. Soon the whine of the engine disappeared and Kara heard only silence. Glancing down at her dusty jeans and stained T-shirt, she wanted to sigh in defeat. But if this was going to be her final evening with Brad, she wasn't going to look like yesterday's leftovers. Glad that Brad was going to pick up a pizza, Kara didn't worry about dinner.

Instead, firming her tired shoulders, she marched into her room and flung open the closet. Narrowing her choices, she tossed a dress onto the bed and then escaped into the bathroom. The bracing water of the shower revived her spirits while making her feel semi-human again. And by the time she finished blow-drying her hair into a soft style, she was beginning to feel distinctly feminine, as well.

Working on a ranch alongside men made her forget that on occasion. But now she applied a light coat of makeup, outlining her eyes in a subtle but distinctive manner, slightly more alluring than usual. It was ridiculous, she knew, but she refused to admit defeat looking like a tired cowhand.

She applied lotion liberally, and her skin glowed as she slipped on a cream-colored silken teddy. Choosing her signature silk, she paused for a moment, wondering if the delicate, frothy dress was appropriate for the evening. Fragile straps held up the scooped neckline and the skirt flowed with endless yards of emerald green material. It was a dress she'd never worn. One that spoke of romantic Southern nights on the veranda.

As though under a magic spell, she reached for her heart-shaped locket and after fastening it, dabbed a few drops of Obsession at her throat. Then she drew in a deep, fortifying breath.

As she walked into the dining room, Kara smelled something wonderful and met Erastus's big smile.

"What in the world?" she asked, seeing dishes piled high with food.

"I had it delivered," he replied. "Hope you don't mind, but I told Brad not to bother with the pizza."

Kara stepped closer, seeing scampi, Oysters Rockefeller, and a divine-looking pasta dish garnished with shiitake mushrooms. "I can't believe you got someone to deliver all this. It looks exquisite."

"And smells even better," Brad added.

She hadn't heard him enter and her eyes widened as she took in his changed appearance. While not formally dressed, he'd showered and changed into snug-fitting stone-washed jeans and a soft-looking charcoal shirt that emphasized his muscular build. Kara felt her breath catch in her throat. How could he continue to surprise her with the effect of his startling looks? By now she should be immune to them. Instead she felt her throat constrict while her stomach danced to an inaudible tune.

Erastus clapped his hands together, diffusing the spell.

"You've even set the table," Kara managed to say, noting the softly burning candles. "I'll get something to drink."

Whipping out a bottle of wine, Erastus applied the corkscrew. "Is this all right?"

"Of course."

Kara finally met Brad's gaze, hoping to telegraph the message that this romantic setting wasn't her idea.

"I'd say that food looks good enough to eat," Erastus announced, forcing them to move as he sat down. "We about ready?"

Brad and Kara took the two remaining chairs. Kara wondered briefly where the other chairs had disappeared to.

Tense silence filled the air as dishes were passed around, the wineglasses filled.

"So, tell me, son, how's all this been affecting your air charter business?"

Brad looked away from Kara, pulled the linen napkin into his lap, then glanced back at Erastus. "It's been rough."

"Worries you, doesn't it?"

"Some."

"It's bound to be on your mind all the time. Hell, a man's business is a big part of who he is. As much a part of you as an arm or a leg. I understand you built your company from the ground up—no fancy investors or anything." Erastus watched Brad as he spoke.

But it was Kara who reacted. Surprise filled her face. "I didn't know that. I assumed that your brother left you a nest egg along with the plane."

Brad shook his head. "The Cessna was the seed. But it took all of my savings for a down payment on another plane and to hire an extra pilot. And everything else was in hock to pay for them."

"A daring move," Erastus said with admiration. "But that's the way a good business is run. Along with some astute planning. I can see both characteristics in the way you've been running the Rocking J, too. Plenty of guts and a lot of well-thought-out plans for the ranch's future." He glanced between them. "But I suppose that's because of you two—each having different things to bring to this partnership."

Kara and Brad sat riveted, staring at him.

Erastus waved his hand in explanation. "Every marriage is a partnership and both people bring some pretty unique aspects to it. Hell, if you were identical in thought and action, you wouldn't be combining the best of both in this operation." His eyes twinkled. "Not to mention how dull that sounds. It's the differences that keep things lively."

Kara kept from sputtering with an effort. *Any livelier and they'd have nuclear potential.*

"I imagine you understand how important Brad's business is to him, don't you, Kara?"

She choked on the wine she'd just swallowed. Fumbling for her napkin, Kara mumbled a response into the downy white folds of material.

"Yep, I thought so," Erastus continued. "You're a smart woman. I expect you're a lot like my Sarah and she was damn near the smartest woman in the world."

Despite her own anxiety, Kara felt a grin tugging at her lips when she heard Erastus's one-sided opinion of his late wife.

"She sure always knew the right things to say and do," Erastus continued. "At least concerning me."

"Like what?" Kara asked softly, wondering what this woman he spoke so highly of did that was so special.

"She always seemed to know what I needed even before I did." Erastus swirled the wine in his glass as the candlelight refracted through the burgundy liquid. "And she was always right."

Brad and Kara were both quiet as their gazes met.

"Say, who's this?" Erastus asked, pointing to Aunt Tillie's portrait.

Kara hadn't even noticed when Brad had moved the painting last. She'd missed their whimsical game of

hide-and-seek. It made her smile to think that Brad
had made one last move. Even if she hadn't detected
it.

"My Great-Aunt Tillie."

"Said with affection. Were you close?" Erastus
asked.

"She was so different than anyone else in my family. Danced strictly to her own tune. I guess you'd call
her eccentric, but she made me believe I could do
anything. Said she hadn't been born in the right time
for that theory to work for her, but that I could ac-
complish most anything. Provided I made my own
rules."

Brad stared at her as she finished speaking, his eyes
too dark in the waning light for her to read.

"Well, the old girl's got character," Erastus conceded as he studied the portrait. "Maybe that's where
you get yours."

Kara shrugged self-consciously, never comfortable
discussing herself. "Everyone thought she was pig-
headed, too."

Brad and Erastus both stared at her without speaking.

Managing a strained smile, Kara offered them more
wine. As she poured, her hand shook just a bit. It was
hard to believe that this would be the last meal she
would share with Brad. Even harder to believe that
their six months together had once seemed like a lifetime imprisonment. Instead the fleeting time left
seemed painfully short. Especially now.

"I imagine your Aunt Tillie had to fight for what
she got," Erastus mused.

"She certainly did." Kara shook her head, remembering. "And even then she was told that it was a

man's world. But she bucked every rule. And it paid off. She started the first women's clinic for the under-privileged at the time. If she hadn't been so determined not to give in to someone else's will, those women wouldn't have had any medical attention. But she paid a price. Her fiancé at the time said he wanted a biddable woman, one who wouldn't stir up such a ruckus. So, while she wrote her own rules and wasn't under anyone's control, she was also alone."

"Never married?" Brad questioned quietly.

Kara met his eyes, refusing to flinch under his regard. "No. Not many men at the time wanted someone as independent as Aunt Tillie."

"Not many men today that can handle that same independence," Erastus commented. "Takes an awful strong man to know that a woman like that remains a challenge, not a threat."

Silence simmered between Brad and Kara, as palpable as the tension that accompanied it.

The room plunged into darkness suddenly, even the candles were blown out by the sudden gust of wind from the open window.

"Brad!" she gasped, sure he'd arranged a repeat performance of the night he'd turned off the electricity. "Did you do this again?"

But he was rising from his chair. "It wasn't me. Nobody's that dumb twice."

He stumbled in the dark, cursing as his shin made contact with the china closet. Kara winced in sympathy as she heard him reach the switch, then hit the doorjamb with his shoulder.

"I'm going to check on the fuses," he said, already moving toward the outside door.

"I'm sure he'll find the problem," she remarked to Erastus.

No answer.

"Erastus? Are you all right?" Worried, she felt her way along in the dark. Not finding him in his chair, she reached for the candlesticks, then slid her hand over the tablecloth until she found the matches.

Striking a match, she inhaled the pungent scent of sulphur as she lit the candles and then searched the dining room in the flickering light. There was no sign of Erastus. Her eyes fell on his vacant chair where a scrap of paper fluttered in the gentle breeze. She picked it up and holding it to the light, read the brief message.

"I'm glad to see I was right. You two belong together. Erastus."

Kara barely had time to register the message, when Brad came back in the room.

"Must be a power outage for the whole area. Our fuses are fine." He glanced around. "Where's Erastus?"

"Gone."

Brad stepped closer. "What's wrong?"

Wordlessly she held out the paper. It took him only seconds to read it. Then his eyes dropped to meet hers.

Warmth and a seed of hope glimmered as she saw the questions in his gaze. The dull anger seemed to have disappeared. Replaced by something that took her breath away. His hand reached toward her face.

The doorbell pealed, then the door flung open and laughter spilled into the entryway. Jerked out of their frozen tableau, Kara and Brad stared as Chuck and Muriel practically danced inside.

"Guess what we've decided?" Chuck asked, his arm looped around Muriel's waist.

"What happened to the lights?" Muriel asked at the same time.

Kara and Brad stared blankly without answering, their own aborted feelings still wound tensely between them.

"It's hard to believe you're speechless," Chuck teased. "I thought you'd have to be comatose for that to happen, old pal."

Brad cleared his throat. "You just caught me by surprise."

"Well, here's an even bigger one." Chuck glanced toward Muriel, a glimpse of tenderness escaping before a huge grin eclipsed his face. "We're getting married!"

"Mom!" Startled, Kara started toward Muriel, shock filling her. But seeing the joy on her mother's face, Kara offered her a warm hug. "Congratulations!" She laughed then. "I guess I'm supposed to say that to Chuck."

"You're right about that," he agreed. "I'm the one to be congratulated. Muriel on the other hand should probably have her head examined."

But Muriel's smile only grew broader, delight making her positively luminescent.

Brad clasped his friend's hand and pumped it up and down. "Damn right. But I'll congratulate you anyway."

Kara reached for Chuck, surprising him with a hug and a tremulous smile. "You've made her happy."

"There's enough to go around," he said softly, glancing significantly at Brad before reaching again for Muriel.

"This calls for champagne," Brad announced. He picked up a candlestick and started toward the wine rack when the lights flickered back on.

"Lights, camera, action," Chuck announced with glee.

Kara stared between her mother and the man she'd decided to marry. It seemed hard to believe that after ten years her refined, elegant mother had chosen a man so different from her late husband.

But perhaps that was why.

Kara had always been saddened that her parents' marriage was a loveless union. Affection, respect, but never a glimpse of passion. And apparently this time around her mother had decided that love was most important.

Chuck trailed after Brad, helping him choose the vintage.

Kara turned to her mother, squeezing her hand. "So he's the one?"

Muriel nodded, then glanced over at the two men. "You're lucky to have found true love the first time around. Not all of us are that fortunate."

Kara couldn't speak for a moment, glancing over toward Brad, seeing the strength of character in his face, the genuine warmth he shared with his friend. "I'm sorry you were so unhappy, Mom."

"I was just too young with your father. He was older and he swept me away." She smiled in memory. "At the time I thought that was very grand, but I didn't know what love really was." She looked at Kara in concern. "That's not to speak badly of him."

"I know, Mom. I could always tell."

Sadness shadowed Muriel's face. "That's not something I wanted for you to know, but it was difficult to hide."

"It didn't make me love Dad any less."

Muriel laughed shakily. "I guess you think I'm pretty crazy to pick someone so different from your father...from myself."

Kara cocked her head. "I don't know. A very wise man told me that the differences keep things lively."

Muriel smiled, the shadows disappearing. "I don't think life with Chuck could possibly be anything less!"

Glancing over at the devil-may-care pilot, Kara had to agree. But part of her still wanted to protect her mother, as she had for so long.

Chuck moved toward them again, the possessiveness in his manner clear. Apparently it was time to relinquish that protectiveness to someone else—someone better suited for the job.

Meeting Brad's gaze across their bent heads, Kara wondered if she too had met her own match. But had her stubbornness ruined it forever?

Chapter Eleven

Brad buried his face deeper into the golden sweep of hair, breathing in that unusual fragrance. Strange how it could permeate even his dreams. Musk and violets trailed all around him, like a sensuous bath of desire. Even better, he could feel Kara's fiery touch as he reached to slide his hands over her satiny curves.

She was all heat and softness, pliant yet responsive. As he'd imagined she would be, as he'd hoped she would be. But in his dream, her touch was tinged with desperation, as well. How could that be? Didn't she know he longed for that touch? Prayed that she would come to see how much she meant to him?

He drew her closer, bending down to suckle her satiny breast, feeling the wild, sweet thrumming of her erratic heartbeat. She tasted of honeysuckle and magnolias, sunshine and smoke. And it drove him crazy. Almost to the point of waking.

But he resisted, knowing this joy couldn't be duplicated if he left the soft cocoon of sleep. His hands stroked the valley of her waist, luxuriated over the hardening tips of her breasts, then wandered to linger over the soft tumble of curls between her legs. He could imagine her opening up to him, the soft warmth he could feel even now, the liquid heat of her response as his touch brought her to a brink she couldn't turn back on.

She wouldn't remind him of practicalities. Instead she would whimper with pleasure, murmur inarticulate words of hot desire, of wishing and wanting.

His leg clamped down over hers, holding this dream image in place while his hands teased that blossom. His consciousness finally penetrated as he realized the hot, slick feel of her was real. Eyes slowly opening, he met her gaze. Hooded with passion, flushed with something akin to pain, she stared at him.

Did that pain mean she didn't want his touch? He wanted to convince her, to ply her with the words to let her know how much she now meant to him. How he wanted to turn that pain to pleasure.

Her mouth opened, but all that emerged was a sigh. Not denial, yet something he couldn't quite read. He wanted to believe it was longing he saw there. Longing that matched his own. His lips moved to capture hers, feeling their needy response, the soft, opening response he'd dreamed of.

Then a huge blast echoed from outside as though a foghorn had erupted. Brad considered ignoring it, but the expression on Kara's face stopped him. Especially when she reminded him what that noise meant. "Birds are out! Oh, Brad, we can't lose our best pairs!"

Galvanized into action, they reached for clothes. Brad was paralyzed for a moment as he saw Kara's body, flushed with arousal, ripe with wanting. Then the blasted horn went off again and they threw on shirts and jeans.

Running to the corral, they each jumped on carts, separating to work more efficiently. And the chase was on. It took the better part of the night, but they finally captured their runaways.

Kara slipped inside the kitchen just as Brad hung up the telephone.

He turned to her with an unreadable expression. "I've got a night flight."

She swallowed her disappointment. "I understand." But she didn't. Couldn't he assign it to another pilot?

"Chuck already asked for the night off. He and Muriel want to celebrate."

"Sure. I understand." Smiling bravely, she met his eyes and was startled by the bleak acceptance there. And desperately hoped she hadn't waited too long to repair things.

WAKING UP EARLY, dressed in her oversize terry robe, Kara was disappointed to see only her mother sipping a cup of coffee. Brad was nowhere in sight. Apparently he hadn't returned home from his late-night flight.

"Morning, dear. I hope we didn't keep you up too late celebrating two nights in a row. But sleep was the last thing on our minds."

Kara swallowed the first comment that came to mind. Instead she kissed her mother's forehead. "It was worth it. But I do need to get going this morning."

"Something special with your birdies?"

Kara made a face. "Don't let Brad hear you call them that. He thinks I'm too attached already."

"He just doesn't know how tenderhearted you are," Muriel replied. "You'd be better off raising something that wouldn't be so painful to slaughter—like tulips or maybe wheat."

Her mother's comment would be funny if it wasn't so true. "I think they grow wheat in Kansas. And we're on the wrong continent for tulips." Kara poured a cup of coffee, relishing the aromatic steam that rose up to greet her. "It's not anything here on the ranch. I have to go into the city."

"Do I want to know any more?"

Wrinkling her forehead, Kara frowned slightly. "Not just yet. If it succeeds, you'll hear about it. If not, I can do without everyone knowing I failed."

Muriel laid a hand over Kara's. Concern filled her expression. "Are things all right between you and Brad?"

Kara had an instant mental vision of her mother ditching her own plans to try to repair Kara's fractured love life. "Like I told you, there's some adjusting to do, that's all. Instead of worrying about me, I think you ought to be out trousseau shopping. You aren't planning to wear flannel jammies on your wedding night, are you?"

Muriel blushed an enchanting shade of rose. "Kara!"

"This from a woman who gave me a see-through nightie for my honeymoon?" Kara rolled her eyes and Muriel giggled. "I've got to dress and make some phone calls."

Going into the den to make her phone calls, where she was assured of privacy, Kara lined up her itinerary. And within a short time, she had changed clothes, retrieving one of her dreaded power suits from the back of the closet. She'd saved the tailored camel and black suit for an unexpected occasion.

Like being buried.

This familiar choking sensation felt close enough. Ignoring the bad memories that came with the uniform, she resolutely fastened on the appropriate gold jewelry, then toed her feet into matching pumps.

Retrieving her leather briefcase, she ignored the qualm that the feel of it in her hand generated. This was a one-time shot, she reminded herself. Not a return to her hated career. And it wasn't for herself this time.

Making sure to avoid Brad, Kara climbed into her car and headed toward the distinctive skyline of downtown Houston—where the power brokers congregated.

An hour after her arrival, Kara was soaring on remembered adrenaline.

"You drive a hard bargain, Mrs. Holbrook." Ronald Harrison, the man across the desk from her, smiled in reluctant appreciation. "I'm not accustomed to tying up this much money in a long-term contract."

Kara clamped the lid shut on her briefcase. "You're also not used to having a steady source of feathers for cleaning microchips. You know as well as I do that most breeders won't allow the birds to be clipped because it stresses them out, preventing them from laying."

He glanced at her quizzically. "And that's not a problem for you?"

"We happen to have a lot of birds who aren't mated yet. They'll be perfect for this."

"If you don't mind me saying so, your talents are wasted out on a ranch." He steepled his hands together. "I've always got a place on my team for a player like you."

Kara acknowledged the quick rush of power, one that had once been seductive. But it was immediately accompanied by the memories of how all-consuming that world was. Her suit suddenly felt constrictive, her need to be back in jeans and a T-shirt overwhelming. She stood up and offered her hand. "Thank you, but I'm happy right where I am." The truth of that statement struck her with renewed force. She had to make this work.

Leaving the offices housed in the dramatic glass Allen Center building, she checked her watch. Just enough time to make her next appointment. Blending easily into the flow of pedestrians that filled the sidewalks, Kara felt the energy that filled the air. Houston was a complex city, one that rebounded constantly, always surprising its critics. And the vitality was intoxicating.

But now Kara knew she'd made the right decision. Her life was wrapped around a man who could easily have ridden the Texas trails a hundred years ago. Uncompromising, daring, he was literally the man of her dreams. But she'd pushed him so far away he couldn't see that. She wondered suddenly what he would do if she told him the truth.

It's a damn good thing this marriage isn't real, because Kara's the last woman on earth I'd marry!

They were difficult words to forget. Still she'd dismissed his air charter business as though it were nothing, forgetting momentarily that it contained an important connection to his late brother. Having turned her back on the corporate world, it hadn't occurred to Kara that Brad's career remained important to him. But Erastus had put the male spin on things and made her realize that she couldn't just assume that Brad should sacrifice his business for the ranch.

Picking up her pace, Kara glanced at the distinctive architecture of the Republic Bank Building. Although a fairly new building, its Gothic lines looked as though they'd been designed a century earlier. It was one of the things she liked so much about the intriguing downtown area—the dramatic differences. Gleaming glass and steel skyscrapers stood next to elegantly classical designs crafted of stone and marble.

Scooting through the revolving door, she stepped inside a blessedly cool interior. Lush green plants decorated the lobby and her heels beat out a staccato on the marble floor. As with many things, appearance was everything and the appearance of this building was rich, luxuriant and distinctive. Taking a deep breath, Kara pushed the elevator button, hoping the contract she planned to negotiate would prove to be just as impressive.

Better than an hour passed before Kara returned to the lobby, but now a huge grin enveloped her face. The terms she'd bargained for in the egg contract were even more lucrative than the one for the feathers. Now she wouldn't have to reverse her decision about slaughtering their animals, yet she wouldn't have to endanger Brad's air charter business to get the money for the mortgage. Her deals guaranteed them a very solid financial footing.

Her grin faded. With so much money coming in from the new contracts she and Brad no longer needed to hold their partnership together because of finances. After the last of their short remaining time was up, they'd be secure enough to split the resources. Sobered by the thought, she didn't see Camilla Kensington until she almost ran into the other woman.

"Kara Lawrence! It *is* you! I didn't think I'd see you back here without a straitjacket." Her shrewd gaze moved to include the briefcase. "Up to your old tricks? Have you been wheeling and dealing again?" Camilla groaned appreciatively. "Don't tell me you want your old job back. I just got the office redecorated!"

Overwhelmed by the rush of words, Kara managed to paste on a serene smile. "As though C.C. would ever rehire me."

Camilla nodded sagely, but not too sympathetically. "He frowns on people walking out on him." She pursed her lips. "Have you moved on to work with the competition?"

"You could say that. I'm working for myself."

"Smart move." Camilla's face showed that she thought just the opposite.

"Not in the corporate world," Kara said. "I'm still not fond of ulcers."

What interest Camilla had evaporated and she glanced pointedly at her Rolex. "Oh, I have to run. Meetings . . . you remember them. We'll have to do lunch *real* soon!" She stepped into the elevator, her bright smile not diminishing as the doors slid closed.

Unfortunately her smile never had reached her calculating eyes.

Exhaling in relief, Kara was glad to move away, feeling as though she'd almost been captured by the enemy. Her next stop didn't require the briefcase and accessories, but it was equally important.

And Kara suspected it would be a lot more rewarding. She fervently hoped so. Because her first two maneuvers had just provided an escape for Brad and an end to their marriage.

BRAD'S PACE DRAGGED as he left his truck and neared the corral. Twilight had descended, painting the sky with a coral blush that competed with deep ridges of purple as the fingers of darkness reached toward the earth. It was a remarkable sunset, one that inspired artists to capture the brilliant colors that feathered together over the horizon.

But Brad couldn't appreciate the beauty. Because inside his coat pocket a contract rested heavily. One he'd thought long and hard about. And one that might blow their existence apart. Still, as had become his habit, he stopped at the entrance of the corral, imagining simpler times. Times when men and women left pretense behind.

A soft whinny broke the silence. Brad shook his head. Fatigue and tension had apparently taken their toll. He was imagining the pleasing sounds of a horse waiting to greet him. A scene he'd pictured in his mind countless times, but not one that fit in with the tense life-style he'd adopted.

The horse pawed the ground, the noise obliterating any notion that it was the product of an overtired imagination. Mesmerized, Brad flicked a glance over the handsome animal. Chestnut that bordered on mahogany, the beast stood at least sixteen hands. He was magnificent.

"Hey, fella," Brad greeted him.

The horse acted equally curious, eyeing the man, as well.

Brad chuckled. "So, who do you belong to?"

"You."

Whirling around, Brad caught the wary look on Kara's face, the inflection in her quiet voice.

Cautiously he reached out to stroke the horse. "What do you mean?"

"He fits in with some of the changes you wanted to make on the ranch." Slowly she approached, hands jammed into tight-fitting jeans.

Brad deliberately kept his gaze fastened on the horse. "I thought you weren't too crazy about those changes."

She shrugged, but he was in tune enough with her to sense the movement. Angling toward her, Brad tried to read the meaning of her unexpected gesture. She remained silent, tossing her hair back as he studied her.

"He's a great horse." Brad slid one hand down the animal's neck.

"Looks like one whose granddaddy might have roamed this land before somebody had to go and invent fences."

"We'd have a hell of a time keeping track of our birds without those fences."

One side of her mouth turned up uncertainly. "Which might not be a bad thing. Since we can't agree what to do about the ostriches."

The contract in his pocket seemed to heat by itself, threatening to ignite the denim of his jacket. It was a ridiculous notion, but the paper represented a volatile solution. Brad's eyes probed hers in the diminishing light. "I've come up with something that might work for all of us—you, me and the birds."

"What do you mean?"

"I've been doing some negotiating." Hoping he wasn't making a mistake, Brad slid the contract out of his pocket.

Kara stared at the trifolded paper, her eyes widening in dismay.

Oh, God, don't tell me we've duplicated the same contracts!

Stomach sinking, she wondered if this, her most impulsive move yet, would push him over the edge.

"I know you can't take the idea of slaughtering the birds," he began, his voice rich and deep, much like the thick night air.

At her sharp intake of breath, he paused, but then continued. "You know how mad I was. But then I realized I hadn't discussed it with you—agreeing to sell the birds for meat. I got to thinking about it and there are other alternatives."

Kara felt a faint tinny buzz near her ears. If she was right and they'd both signed obligations to provide the same materials from the flock, he would kill her. Deliberately she took a deep breath, but its effects didn't reach her paralyzed brain.

Brad slowly unfolded the paper. "I know I didn't talk this out with you, but I wasn't sure I could negotiate the terms. Or if they'd be terms we could live with."

Kara gripped the corral railing, wanting to scream at him to get it over with. Show her proof of just how mismatched they were—neither able to trust the other enough to communicate. What were they going to do with duplicate contracts? Other than get sued.

"But," he said slowly, drawing out the words, "I think you'll like this idea. The birds won't have to be killed, or even hurt."

There it was. The two of them should at least get a booby prize for being the biggest idiots in the world.

"And there are a lot of zoos in the world needing our birds. It's an international market, one with more potential than I realized."

Zoos? Did he say zoos?

The ringing in her ears faded, as she spoke carefully. "You negotiated a contract to sell some of the birds to zoos?"

He nodded, turning back to stroke the horse's mane. "What do you think?"

Relief burst through her, knowing they had enough stock to fulfill all the contracts. "I think that's wonderful."

Surprised, he slanted his face toward hers. "You do? Even though I didn't discuss it with you first?"

Kara jammed her hands into her pockets, stalling. "Is that such a bad thing? I mean, sometimes you just have to do what your impulses tell you to."

A light flickered in his eyes. "Are you trying to tell me that you have more surprises for me than the horse?"

"I'm trying to *not* tell you," she admitted, pleased to see that his hand still lingered on the horse's mane, the pleasure on his face too rooted to vanish at the prospect of her surprise. "But we have contracts for feathers and eggs, as well."

"Why doesn't that surprise me?"

"As long as it doesn't make you angry. After all, it wasn't in the business plan."

An indefinable light lit his eyes. "No, I guess it wasn't." He turned back to the horse. "What made you think to buy him?" Brad asked softly.

She considered her options, then settled on the truth. "Because I thought he'd make you happy."

Brad's hand paused as he stroked the horse's satiny flank. Then he caught her gaze, refusing to relinquish it. "I think it might take more than that."

Tension stretched between them, taut and nearly visible. Struggling with a sense of wonder, Kara didn't know if she dared believe what he'd left unspoken. Did he mean that he needed someone in his life? Maybe her?

She swallowed, watching as his eyes darkened even further. Then he dropped the hand that rested on the horse. Moving toward her with purpose, one arm shot out as he pulled her close.

Kara didn't even consider resisting.

Her mouth opened to accept a kiss that held all the fire she'd dreamed of. Bone-melting, heart-rendering heat.

His lips slid along hers as his tongue danced and mated with hers. Her blood thinned, her heart soared and electricity fused her disjointed senses into a lightning rod of acceptance.

Kara melted closer against him, feeling the thrust of his arousal, the solid width of his chest as it connected with her breasts. One hand slid beneath her T-shirt to caress the length of her back while the other cupped her neck. Each fingerprint seared her sensitized skin, while her body dissolved beneath his touch. Liquid heat signaled that this time they would tolerate no interruptions.

As if in response to her silent thoughts, Brad slid his hand up the sensitive flesh of her rib cage, then caressed her breast beneath her skimpy bra. The nipple jumped to attention, followed by her sigh of acceptance.

Certain that if they hadn't been standing outside at the corral, Brad would have whipped off her shirt, Kara instead encouraged his hands to memorize her body while he nibbled at her throat, then framed her face in his hands.

A sound finally penetrated through her drugged senses. A truck horn honked loudly and insistently.

Brad swore with equal vehemence.

Kara pulled her shirt into place as the pickup swung into the driveway.

"I'll get rid of them," Brad promised, his voice low and determined.

Meeting his gaze, Kara tried to slow the rapid breathing he'd caused, but the look in his eyes only made it intensify. "Hurry."

Like a man with a mission, Brad strode toward the truck. But Chuck and Muriel scrambled out before he could reach them.

"Did you tell her?" Chuck asked Brad, a big grin on his face.

"Well, yes, but—"

"Darling, I'm so glad everything's worked out," Muriel gushed as she reached to hug Kara. "Chuck told me all about the contract for the zoos. That's wonderful! I knew Brad would think of something once he knew what a tenderhearted little minx you are. We have to celebrate." She pointed to the bottles of champagne Chuck held up in both hands.

"But—"

"It's not—"

"We're not taking no for an answer," Muriel announced. "It's about time you got some good news. And after all this time that Chuck and Brad have been flying double shifts, we plan to celebrate big!"

Laughing at something Chuck whispered in her ear, Muriel led the way to the house.

Brad and Kara stared at each other in dismay.

"Maybe they won't stay long?" Kara asked hopefully.

"And maybe pigs really do fly," Brad responded glumly. "We'll have a few drinks and then suggest going dancing. When they're ready to leave, we'll back out."

Kara looked dubious. "You think that'll work?"

Brad sighed. "If luck's with us. Considering how things have gone so far, I wouldn't count on it." Brad put an arm around her and they started toward the house.

Shrugging, Kara murmured, "How long can a few drinks take?"

Chapter Twelve

The stars stood solidly in the black canopy, along with a moon so full it looked as though it had been painted over the evening sky. Kara and Brad stared at each other across the table, longing filling their faces.

The champagne had just been an appetizer, followed by a full-blown, Texas-sized barbecue. Muriel had pulled out all the stops, insisting on all the fixings. But Kara and Brad's plates were both nearly full, remaining untouched as the pressure between them mounted.

"How about dancing?" Brad suggested, thinking he might pull his friend aside and tell him to take Muriel and get lost.

"Great idea," Chuck agreed. "I'll turn on the CD player."

"No, I meant go somewhere."

"When we can dance under the stars?" Chuck held out his hand to Muriel, but before he turned, Brad thought he recognized an almost hidden smirk. Deciding it must be a trick of the moonlight, Brad dismissed the idea. Even Chuck wouldn't be that rotten.

"Your plan doesn't seem to be working," Kara whispered.

Brad suspected that every fate in the universe was poised against them. "At this rate, we'll be watching the sun come up with them."

Chuck and Muriel swirled close, obviously enthralled with each other.

"I could dance all night," Chuck mimicked.

"Well, I can't," Brad muttered as he stood up and then held out his hand to Kara. "We're going for a walk."

The sky seemed to open up even further, reminiscent of a time when it had stretched out across the vast, unfettered state with no artificial boundaries.

But they'd barely crossed over toward the breeding pens when Chuck and Muriel caught up with them.

Suddenly suspicious, Brad turned and stared at his friend. "Are you following us?"

"Like we don't have anything better to do?" Chuck's voice was convincingly incredulous. "I thought we were celebrating."

Muriel took his arm. "Maybe we should—"

Suddenly a loud *boom* sounded out across the breeding pen—two short calls and one long. The male ostrich stretched himself to his full height, repeating the booms.

Kara and Brad glanced at each other as Muriel and Chuck fell silent. The booms precipitated the mating ritual. This pair's last attempt hadn't been successful. While Kara wanted them to succeed, she wasn't sure this was the best time to watch.

The drab-looking hen didn't seem prepared to run in flight this time. Instead she watched the male as he started his courting. The booms continued filling the air as the male began showing off to impress the hen. Dropping to his "knees," he rolled back and forth, swaying from left to right with his head down, raising first one wing and then the other. For human observers, it was a comical dance.

But as the hen watched, her wariness disappeared, and her interest increased.

The bowing and rolling of the cock continued as the courtship dance progressed. Heat flushed Kara's skin as she watched. Willing herself to back away, instead she watched the birds under the guise of making sure they were safe. But she was overtly conscious of Brad's presence, the ritual they were observing, the sensations the man at her side created, the culmination she wanted to happen. One that had been denied too long.

Forgetting Chuck and Muriel, forgetting anything but each other, the air roiled around them, thick, constrictive, confining.

A trill of laughter from near the house penetrated long enough to let them know that Chuck and Muriel had blessedly left them alone.

"Is that us?" Brad asked, gesturing to the birds. "Wanting each other, but fighting it until it almost couldn't happen?"

Kara's throat closed. Then her hands reached out as she had wanted to do for so long. Touching the slant of his jaw, then burying her hands in his hair, she breathed in his clean scent, knowing it was one she would never forget. Raising her eyes to his, she saw them unveiled for the first time. "It was," she whispered, "but it doesn't have to be."

Chuck's truck horn blasted through the quiet as the vehicle's engine roared to life. Glancing up in time to see Muriel waving goodbye, Kara's and Brad's eyes jerked back to stare at each other.

Of one accord they moved toward the house. Only a few lights had been left on, burning lowly like beacons. Brad extinguished them, then pulled Kara's hand into his as he moved toward the bedroom.

"No more interruptions," he declared. "Even if it means locking every door in the house and boarding up the windows."

"It works to keep out hurricanes."

"Then it probably wouldn't stop Chuck. But I don't have time to dig a moat."

Breathlessly she agreed. Time was the enemy, one they had to conquer. Pushing away the thought of how little remained of their allotted time, Kara walked eagerly toward the master bedroom.

The room seemed suddenly different, not familiar territory at all. Though they'd played out the game for some time, the rules had suddenly changed.

Ridiculously nervous, Kara paused by the doorway as Brad stepped inside. Hearing a thud, followed by a low curse, she grimaced as she remembered what she'd done.

"What the . . . ?" Brad's surprised voice growled in the dark.

Then a reluctant chuckle emerged as he reached around and guided Kara past the offending object. His recliner stood at half-mast where she'd left it when he'd come home. She'd been in the midst of her move in their game. Impatient to see his reaction to the horse, she'd forgotten all about it.

Until now.

But she could taste his smile as Brad pulled her down with him to the soft pillowing of their bed and captured her lips.

"You're something, you know that?" His hand stroked the silken strands of her hair, then smoothed over the curve of her cheek to rest just beneath her kiss-swollen mouth. Moonlight spilled in the oversize bay window, illuminating their faces, trailing over the room.

"So are you, Brad Holbrook." The need to tell him that she loved him was fierce, but it was overshadowed by sensation as he kissed the hollows of her throat, the tender flesh behind her ears. As his lips moved down her neck, she shivered in anticipation.

His eyes burned as he leaned back long enough to peel off his shirt, then follow the motion by removing her shirt, as well. He paused for only a moment as the wispy, silken bra stood in his way. Then in a second it too was gone. Kara wasn't sure whether the gasp she heard was her own or his. The cool night air puckered her nipples as the moonlight played over her pale flesh. But Brad's hands were achingly warm as they circled her breasts.

Liquid warmth stabbed her insistently, especially when his mouth replaced his hands. Moaning her need and her desire, Kara writhed beneath his touch, wanton now that he had found the snap to her jeans and dispatched them quickly.

Brad sucked in his breath as Kara's flawless body unfolded beneath him. Only a scrap of her signature silk remained. She was as perfect as he'd imagined and in one quick movement he bared the final obstacle.

Satin and silk blended in a sinuous dance. The fragment of silk he still clutched in one hand, the satin of her skin as he leaned into her welcoming arms.

Feeling her hands fumble with the fastening to his jeans, he drew a ragged breath. Her delicate hands grazed his engorged arousal and he couldn't contain an answering groan. Helping her remove his jeans was a sweet torture for them both.

Then they were both naked, baring unadorned skin that yearned to be together. Brad obliged, reveling in the feel of her against him, the arch of her hip, the valley of her curving waist, the swell of her breasts spilling against his chest.

His hands roamed, unable to get enough of her sweet scent, the taste of her skin. Overwhelmed by her reactions, he savored each one.

A prisoner of his touch, Kara arched against his sure but gentle hands. When his fingers reached to probe the soft folds of flesh that centered her sensations, she bit back a cry. But hearing it, he closed his lips over hers while he continued the magic.

Meeting his gaze, she saw the light in his expression, the tenderness in his eyes and she melted even more. But it was her heart that warmed, as well. Eager for all of him, she sighed as his hands slid over her thighs, down her calves as he positioned himself.

Once inside her, Brad wondered how he could have waited so long for this moment. She was so sure, so right. How could he have not known? Then she moved against him.

Satin and silk turned to fire and wonder.

When an all-consuming shudder shook him, he felt Kara's answering response as her breasts crushed into his chest, her ragged breathing matching his own.

Pulling back, he watched the moonlight play over her features, cherishing them, memorizing them. Wondering if they would remain his, or if she would leave with the freedom the contracts he'd negotiated would provide.

SUNSHINE REPLACED the silver bath of moonlight and Kara stretched beneath the warm, golden beams. Disappointed to find Brad already up and out of bed, still she smiled as she remembered how they'd occupied the hours till nearly dawn. Knowing if she glanced in a mirror that she would resemble a smug Cheshire cat, Kara padded instead to the bath and swung open the shower door.

Aunt Tillie stared at her.

Laughing out loud, Kara threw back her mane of disheveled hair as she wondered what her dear, departed aunt must be thinking. She was probably smiling down from heaven, no doubt deciding that her niece was having a far better time than she ever had.

Two strong arms reached around her as Brad bent and gently nipped her earlobe. "She gets around, doesn't she?"

Kara tried to look properly severe. "Aunt Tillie never traveled this much when she was alive."

"Oh, but what she missed." Brad turned her to face him, nudging her closer.

He wore only a towel, which she found ridiculously easy to steal.

Brad nuzzled her neck. "There's a price to pay for stealing, my sweet."

She tried to look nonchalant, but blew it when she started giggling.

He shook his head in mock severity. "Ah, I see you're not properly repentant. The penalty goes up."

Her gaze traveled downward, her lips twitching. "So I see."

Brad reached behind her, removed Aunt Tillie's portrait and shoved it onto the counter. Then they were inside the shower stall, the door closed, the water running.

But they created the steam on their own.

Brad picked up the soap, rubbing it over Kara's back, trailing it along the back of her thighs, then turning her so that she faced him. Soaping her hips, then the swell of her stomach, she sucked in her breath as he moved upward, taking great care to work up a lather around her breasts.

But the lather didn't stop there.

Water-slickened bodies slid together with precision that defied the duration of their time together. As Brad picked her up, she wrapped her legs around him, her fingers clutching his shoulders, her mouth fastened to his.

Water sluiced over them, washing away the soap, bringing unexpected heights of sensation. Mouths fused together, Kara could taste the mineral zest of the water, along with the flavor that was Brad's alone.

Long strands of her wet hair dangled between their chests, providing a provocative tug and pull between the spray of the shower and the movement of their bodies. Throwing her head back, Kara felt Brad nip lightly at her neck and released a groan she couldn't contain.

His thrusts deepened and Kara welcomed each one, knowing that she was climbing . . . climbing. The mirrors fogged, dimming their images. And the steam continued to build.

IT WAS MORE THAN AN HOUR later before Kara emerged from the bedroom. She looked guiltily toward the kitchen. Even though she was a married woman, and now a very sated one, she still felt self-conscious knowing her mother would have guessed why they were so late in leaving their room.

But she was surprised by the empty kitchen. Even more surprised to see that it looked almost deserted. No coffee had been made, not even any leftover breakfast food or dishes remained on the counter or table.

Frowning, Kara scanned the room again, trying to see if she'd overlooked something. Then the note on the refrigerator door caught her attention. Plucking it from beneath the Texas-shaped magnet, Kara started reading it when Brad trailed in, kissing her neck as she tried to make sense of the note.

When his caresses evoked no reaction, he stared at her quizzically. "Tired of me already?"

Silently she passed him the note.

Brad read it quickly, his brows rising. "They've eloped? Beauty and the Beast?"

"I guess they were more serious than I realized. I know they told us they were getting married, but I assumed they'd be engaged for a while." Disoriented, Kara clutched the refrigerator door.

Brad stopped reading the note and examined her pale face. "You don't sound very happy for them."

"I am. But it's such an important occasion. And they just took off so—"

"Impulsively?" Brad asked wryly.

She made a face at him. "Did you happen to notice where they were going?"

Brad dropped his gaze to finish reading the note, then hooted. "Vegas?"

Kara nodded. "Can you believe them?"

Brad skimmed a thumb up the curve of her cheek and then down over her lips. "I don't know. Some of the best marriages start out that way."

Her voice was low, speculative. "Do they?"

What they'd left unresolved the day before now came rushing back with a vengeance.

Brad took a deep breath. "The contract for the zoos will give us enough money for our buyout agreement to kick in soon."

Releasing them from their obligation to each other, unless he wanted to stay with her as much as she wanted him to. Kara searched his face. "I never did get around to telling you the details of the egg and feather contracts."

"No," he responded slowly, "you didn't."

Briefly she outlined the contracts she'd negotiated the previous day, at last glad for all the extra birds Brad had purchased. Then she paused, allowing a brooding silence to develop. What if he took advantage of this opportunity to leave? If he actually enacted that buyout agreement? Feeling her heart shattering, Kara tried to believe that wouldn't happen, that the feelings they had shared meant more to him than that.

Brad's eyes didn't leave hers. "In other words, there's no need at all to keep the agreements intact. With the windfall, we're financially sound. We can end ... the partnership with a buyout as soon as the time in the addendum is up and we've satisfied Erastus's clause."

Feeling that short time ticking away, wishing she didn't have to, Kara nodded her agreement, keeping a glint of tears well hidden. She couldn't even imagine which one of them would get the ranch, because in her mind ... in her heart ... it belonged to them both.

The phone rang, a shrill intrusive interruption.

Kara stared at it resentfully, but Brad responded with a heavy undertone to his words. "You'd better get it."

Wishing she was doing anything else, Kara snatched up the receiver and listened for a few moments while Brad watched intently.

"Hi, Mom. Yes, we got your note. Congratulations. We're ... both very happy for you." She listened again, watching Brad watch her. "You aren't coming back here? Of course, Chuck's apartment. Yes, I'll tell Brad. Have a great honeymoon. I know you have to get back soon because of Chuck's schedule, still ... have a wonderful time. I love you, too, Mom."

Slowly Kara hung up the receiver. "She won't be coming back here," she repeated unnecessarily. "They'll be living at Chuck's apartment."

"I didn't think she'd keep staying at the ranch."

Kara pressed a hand to her forehead. "Of course not." And now there was no need to play out the charade, unless Erastus showed up unexpectedly. Hoping for a declaration of his feelings, Kara watched Brad.

But he turned away abruptly. "I won't have time for breakfast. It'll be a tight schedule covering for Chuck." His eyes lingered on her face for a moment longer, then he disappeared.

Sinking against the wall, Kara wondered if he already regretted their night together. And if he was planning to take advantage of the new financial situation to extricate himself from the marriage.

KARA WATCHED OUT the window for a sign of Brad's truck. He was late. Far later than he should have been. Her stomach clenched as she wondered if he would return to his old habits of sleeping at the office now. After what they'd shared, her bed would be incredibly empty.

The house seemed far too lonely with Chuck and her mother gone. More though since Brad wasn't here. Frustrated, she wondered what he would have done if she'd confessed her feelings, just blurted out that she loved him. Would he have reciprocated? Or run even faster to escape?

Sighing, she closed the shutters, shutting away the reminder of how late it was. Her eyes fell on the carefully set table. Two settings of their best china, along with champagne flutes and the good silver decorated the table. And of course she'd added fresh flowers from the garden along with fragrant tapers of beeswax. It was a flagrantly romantic setup. One that now made her feel inordinately foolish. Leaning forward to blow out the candles, she paused as she heard the distinctive sounds of Brad's truck.

Prepared to explain away the table, she wasn't prepared for the way he breezed in, then pulled her close, kissing her before she could speak, before she could think.

His lips were hungry, commanding. And she fell under his spell immediately. Greedily their mouths fused together, a searching reunion that ignited them both.

Gasping when she pulled away, the air whooshing from her lungs, Kara met his gaze, then blurted out the first thing she thought of. "You're late."

"I've been busy. With Chuck out, we had a tight schedule."

He turned away for a moment and she caught her breath, still winded from his powerful embrace.

His eyes took in the table and then drifted back to her.

"I thought you might be hungry," she offered lamely.

He didn't comment. Instead he reached for the corkscrew she held out.

Scrambling desperately for something to say, she asked the first thing that popped into her head. "Did you hear from Chuck today?"

He shook his head. "No, but considering the circumstances, I didn't expect to."

Kara flushed hotly. "Of course."

Blindly she turned away.

But Brad reached out for her. "I spoke to the attorney today."

Kara froze. She'd thought he might want to end their relationship. But so soon . . .

"I told him that you should have first right of buy-out."

Kara whirled around. "You should have the ranch! It's been your lifelong dream. You've always loved it." *But do you love me? Enough to stay together even though we don't have to?*

"What about your freedom? Your need not to be controlled?" he asked, his voice husky, almost gruff.

She shrugged. "Freedom's just a part of happiness." Deliberately she glanced away. "And happiness is tied up with all kinds of other things."

Brad ran his hand over her bare arm, pausing just above her elbow, then reaching with his other hand to tip up her chin, forcing her to look at him. "What kinds of things?"

But the knot in Kara's throat was too great, the need to tell him overpowering.

He fisted several strands of her hair, letting them sift through his fingers as the candlelight caught their golden highlights. "Your hair's like you. All silk and satin. Sunshine and promises."

Kara bent her head. Could she confess her love and accept that she loved him even if he didn't return that feeling? Could she deliberately step into the same painful relationship that her mother had with her father? Eyes blazing, she raised her chin, then met his gaze.

"What is happiness, Kara?" Brad moved closer, trapping her against the refrigerator. "Is it what Erastus found with Sarah? Or Chuck with Muriel?"

Cold steel burned through her silk shirt, but Kara could only blink at the intensity in Brad's eyes, at odds with the calmness of his voice. "It's . . . it's . . ."

"Is it finding that impulse and stolidity go hand in hand? Or that it doesn't matter that you're as different as two people can be? Or that you care more about another person's happiness than your own?"

Kara swallowed. "Do you . . . care?"

"Do you?" he countered, his voice as deep as the emotions she swam in.

The house around them was ominously silent. No one was left to interrupt or to put on a show for.

Kara felt every ridge of his muscled body close to hers. "Now we don't *have* to stay married."

His voice was husky, seeded with something she couldn't define. "No."

Her eyes met his. "Now we can decide what we *want,*" she said softly.

"And what is that, Kara?"

She reached up to touch the curl of ebony hair near his brow. "I didn't think you were a slow study."

He sucked in a deep breath. "You really are something. But you'd better be sure," he warned. "Because I love you and I don't intend to let you go."

Kara was glad for his arms surrounding her, holding her against the refrigerator door because she was suddenly limp, boneless. She cleared her throat. "Would you mind repeating that?"

"I said, don't even think of wiggling out of this contract, *Mrs. Holbrook,* because you aren't going anywhere."

"The other part," she insisted breathlessly, not certain she hadn't imagined those magic words.

"I love you," he said, leaning close, then giving her a gentle shake. "Even though you're the most impulsive, harebrained woman I've ever met."

Kara twined her arms around his neck. "Keeps you from being too persnickety."

"Is that your way of saying I plan ahead too much?" he asked, reaching into his pocket.

Her eyes dropped to the small jeweler's box he held in one hand. "What...?"

But he released her and snapped open the lid on the velvet box. Seeing what it contained, Kara couldn't speak.

Smiling, Brad reached inside and slipped out the ring. It was a perfect replica of her cubic zirconium wedding ring with only a few minor alterations. This one was fashioned from elegant rose quartz and soft, brushed gold. Next to it was a simple wedding band of the same brushed gold.

Speechless, Kara watched as Brad slipped the replica onto her finger.

"I know it's not from Vegas, but I hope it'll do," he said, still holding her hand, then dropping a kiss on her fingers.

Kara felt the warmth in her heart bubbling over to a bursting point. "I can't believe you did this."

"And I can't believe you're mine."

Kara responded with the only answer that fit. Tenderly she kissed the underside of his jaw, then raised up to capture his lips. He responded hungrily, as though afraid she might disappear beneath his touch.

Candlelight flickered over their faces as Brad reached behind them to turn off the switch on the overhead light.

"Didn't rig the fuse box again, did you?" she asked, her lips curling upward.

"Don't tempt me," he growled. His eyes swept over her. "On second thought, tempt me."

"I love you," she responded fiercely, wanting him to know the depth of that feeling.

He answered her simply with a kiss. One so tender yet powerful that she sank against him with a sigh. One that lengthened with the shadows of night.

Chapter Thirteen

Kara held the envelope up to the light, puzzled to see that it had been returned. It was one of the invitations they'd sent out to their friends and relatives. She and Brad had decided to renew their hasty wedding vows and wanted their loved ones to share in the special event. This invitation was addressed to Erastus.

But it was the abrupt wording that the post office had stamped across the envelope that threw Kara.

Deceased. Return to sender.

Hearing Brad walk up behind her, wordlessly she handed the invitation to him.

"It must be some kind of mistake," Brad muttered. "It's been a few weeks since we've heard from Erastus, but..." He turned the envelope over in his fingers, as though weighing the cream-colored ivory. "I'll call him."

When he reached a disconnect recording, Brad looked up the address of the attorney who had drawn up the papers for Erastus.

Concern lined Kara's face. "Let's both go talk to him."

Brad didn't argue.

In a short time they reached the attorney's office and a smiling secretary showed them in. Brian Thomas, the attorney, greeted them warmly, although he looked a bit puzzled.

"What can I do for you?" Brian asked, after offering them chairs. "Something come up in the contract that needs clarification?"

Kara held up the returned invitation. "No, this came in today's mail. I know it must be some kind of mistake."

The attorney took the invitation, read the printed wording from the post office, then carefully took off his glasses. "I thought you knew."

"But it can't be," Kara insisted.

"He was quite elderly, Mrs. Holbrook. Full of spirit to be sure, but still not any spring chicken. It was sudden, but peaceful. A heart attack in his sleep."

Kara's eyes misted over.

"I didn't realize you knew him that well," Brian continued, still baffled. "I thought you just met him when you bought the ranch."

"We did," Brad answered shortly.

"Then I am confused," the attorney replied. "He died the day after all the contracts were finalized at the closing—just a few days after you took occupancy of the ranch."

Brad and Kara stared at each other in shock, mouths falling open in disbelief.

"But that was over six months ago," Brad answered slowly.

"Yes, I guess it was. Strange you just finding out now."

"I'll say," Brad muttered.

"You know Erastus was right about one thing," Brian commented.

"What was that?" Brad asked, meeting Kara's eyes, recognizing her disbelief and telegraphing back his own message for her to hold her silence.

"He told me that you two were meant for each other—that he hadn't seen a couple so perfect since he and Sarah met. And since you got married in order to buy the ranch, he must have been right. After all, you haven't questioned the addendum since the papers were signed. I wondered how he determined all this on the face of one meeting, but he was a sly old dog."

The shock multiplied. Erastus *knew* all along!

Kara's eyes widened. "But—"

"Can you tell us where he's buried?" Brad interrupted.

The attorney hesitated for only a moment. "I can't see that it would do any harm. Since I went to the service I can tell you the name of the cemetery and where it's located."

Within a few minutes Kara and Brad were back outside, the directions to the cemetery jotted down on a piece of paper in Brad's pocket.

"We can't have imagined everything," Kara breathed.

"I'd like to see this for myself," Brad agreed, disturbed by the attorney's insistence that Erastus had indeed died on that exact date.

It didn't take long to find the small cemetery, since it wasn't far from the ranch. Ancient magnolia trees flanked the drive, scenting the air sweetly. Lush, like most of Houston's countryside, still this place seemed greener, brighter. Weeping willows trailed near a pond afloat with ducks.

"It sounds sort of irreverent, but this is a great place," Kara commented in a hushed voice.

"No need to whisper," Brad added dryly.

"Oh, right." Her voice strengthened. "I guess we won't be disturbing anyone."

He quirked an eyebrow, but didn't comment as they walked side by side on the paths, finally spotting a tombstone inscribed with the Jones's name. It was a double headstone, one side bearing Sarah's name.

The other inscribed with Erastus's.

And the date of his death was just over six months ago.

"But how? Why?" Kara knelt next to the stone, tracing the chiseled lettering.

"No one else ever seemed to see him," Brad mused.

Kara glanced up, remembering. "I know the night he came to dinner I thought it was strange that my mother hadn't run into him. And then he disappeared so mysteriously when the lights went out."

"You realize this means we've owned the ranch all along, marriage or no marriage," Brad said slowly.

Kara's eyes met and held his. "But if we hadn't thought we *had* to stay together, we'd have probably split up right away."

"And the old man always seemed to show up when we were ready to call it quits." Brad studied the markings, trying to make sense of what they'd learned.

Wonder filled her voice. "It was as though he knew when things were at a breaking point, and he appeared to make sure that we stayed together."

"Where do you suppose he's been the past few weeks?"

"I think he's free at last to join Sarah," she replied softly, her fingers still resting on the blush-colored granite stone.

"Now that he knows that we don't need him?" Brad asked, his voice husky, still unable to believe that he'd almost let this woman go. Glad he'd come to his senses in time.

"Our cupid guardian angel can finally rest," she agreed, meeting Brad's eyes as they both rose slowly and turned away from the neatly manicured area. Fragrant peach roses bloomed nearby, accompanied by a rush of wild honeysuckle.

Kara started down the pathway, but Brad paused. "You go ahead. I'll be along."

She walked away as he turned to study the marker once more.

"Thanks, Erastus. I owe you. Forever." Then Brad turned to rejoin Kara, imagining the older man's wink and the accompanying smile from his Sarah.

"THIS IS SILLY," Kara protested, looking at her reflection in the full-length mirror.

Muriel pursed her lips. "You're right, dear. None of these dresses suit you." She fingered the flounces on the last two choices, one dress that was covered in rows of lace, the other in ostentatious beading. "And I did so want you to have exactly what you liked."

Kara stared at the pile of dresses they'd brought home on approval. "There might be one that would work."

Studying the dresses strewn out on the bed, Muriel frowned. "Which one?"

Pushing aside the bow that overwhelmed the dress she wore, Kara walked over to the trunk at the end of the bed. The idea had been nagging at her all week. She propped open the lid and dug to the bottom, carefully lifting out an ancient box, tied with a faded blue ribbon.

Muriel's face lit with recognition as Kara separated the tissue paper and held up a fragile-looking dress, anxious to see her mother's reaction.

"Aunt Tillie's wedding gown!" Muriel exclaimed. "I'd forgotten all about it. But of course it was with her other things she wanted you to have." She reached out to touch the beautiful pale peach silk. "Even though she never wore it herself."

Kara stood up and held the gown against her body, pivoting for Muriel's inspection. "What do you think?"

"I think Aunt Tillie would be thrilled to know you wore it. You were the closest thing she had to a daughter. Even though she was in her eighties when you entered your teens, I think she saw all of her dreams coming true in you. You were the only one in the family whose spunk matched hers."

"I wonder if there's a headpiece." Kara reached into the chest and found instead the advertisement that accompanied the dress, one that had been carefully cut from a turn-of-the-century fashion template. Chuckling, she held it up for her mother to see. "And look what the bride's carrying instead of a bouquet."

Muriel's eyes widened as she studied the photograph and the accompanying description. "A white ostrich feather fan?"

"It was all the rage," Kara mimicked in her best Katharine Hepburn voice.

"Sounds like an outfit made to order," Muriel agreed ruefully.

"You're sure you and Chuck don't want to renew your vows with us?" Kara asked, not wanting to exclude them, yet secretly wishing this ceremony could be hers and Brad's alone.

Muriel held up her hands in mock horror. "Heavens no! Once was enough for us. Besides, we knew what *we* were getting into."

Kara lifted one eyebrow. "Touché, Mom."

Muriel grinned. "Besides, by now your arranged marriage has had time to take."

Kara spluttered. "Did Chuck tell—"

"Hardly. He still doesn't know that I know." Her grin turned wicked. "But it'll keep him on his toes."

Shaking her head slowly, Kara measured her mother with growing respect. "I'm not sure what to think of you."

Muriel's smile was filled with love. "Don't forget. I've always been able to read you. And keeping secret the man you loved enough to marry just wasn't your style."

"Can we come in yet?" Chuck called from the hallway.

Kara quickly stashed the gown back inside the box. "We'll be out in a minute!" She glanced at her mother, lowering her voice. "I know it sounds stupid, but I don't want Brad to see the dress until the ceremony."

Muriel leaned forward and kissed her cheek. "I think it's sweet." Reaching one hand out, she pushed a strand of hair away from Kara's temple. "You're truly in love now, aren't you?"

Grinning, Kara reached out to hug her. "You'd know."

Arm in arm they marched out to the living room, where Brad's recliner was back in full prominence. Chuck stood in front of Aunt Tillie's portrait. "Since Brad doesn't like having her portrait around, we'll take the Aunt Tillie off your hands. I don't mind having a woman watching me all the time."

Brad stepped forward. "Nope. The picture means too much to Kara."

Her eyes swung toward him, shaped into circles of surprise.

"Besides, I've grown kind of fond of the old girl myself," he added, the smile that started in his eyes matching Kara's.

Chuck left Muriel's side to walk in front of the portrait, staring as Aunt Tillie's eyes continued to follow him. "Good idea, Brad." His voice broadened as he shook off an involuntary shudder. "Just so long as you don't take her with you on the honeymoon."

BRAD SEARCHED the crowded area for a glimpse of his bride. Tented awnings protected long tables of food and the bar flowed freely. While Japanese lanterns had been hung to provide light when darkness approached, it hadn't been necessary to decorate with much else. The grounds themselves provided the flowers.

Brad couldn't believe he was so caught up in the ceremony itself. He'd always thought it was something only for the bride, with the groom as a necessary prop. But now he awaited Kara's arrival as anxiously as their guests. She'd refused to let him see her gown and had made him sleep on the couch the night before. Firmly but gently, she informed him this time it was going to be a real wedding and a real marriage.

And just that short separation had him aching for her.

But she'd kept him at bay all through the morning and early afternoon, as well, telling him, through messengers, that it was bad luck to see the bride before the wedding.

Wiping his perspiring palms against his legs, he wished she hadn't picked now to go formal and traditional on him. He missed his impulsive wife.

The tempo of the music changed, then the definitive strains of the wedding march filtered through the air. The pastor winked at him in encouragement, but Brad barely managed a smile. Give him Vegas any day.

Then Kara appeared and he discarded that thought as foolish, even stupid. All the nuisance of the ceremony disappeared as a rush of love, wild and sweet, filled him. She was so beautiful it made his heart beat faster.

Was she really his?

Then she lifted her eyes, their brilliant green seeking him out. What he saw there reassured him and he stood up taller, proud as she walked surely and

smoothly toward him. A swift stab of possessiveness
made him want to shout to everyone that this incredible woman was his. And that, luckily, he hadn't been
fool enough to lose her.

His eyes swept over the gown she'd chosen. The pale
peach silk looked antique, as though preserved from
some other age. A veil of tulle, held on her brow by a
garland of orange blossoms, set off her exquisite face,
then cascaded over her shoulders and down the back
to cover the gown's train. Sucking in his gut, he knew
there had never been a bride more beautiful.

As his gaze swept over her, his lips lifted in unexpected amusement. In her right hand she carried a
white ostrich fan. He wasn't sure what kind of fashion statement she was making, but he loved her originality. Then it struck him—the antique gown. It must
belong to Tillie. Kara had dropped a few hints and
he'd expected to see Tillie's portrait on display, but
apparently it was the old girl's dress that was to be part
of the day.

Kara kept her gaze trained on Brad, thrilled to see
the smile reaching his eyes. She drew in her breath at
the sight of him—so handsome and commanding as he
waited for her. He'd chosen a well-tailored black tux
and a stiffly starched white shirt that set off his dark
good looks. Her heart swelled, still unable to believe
he loved her as much as she did him.

The music tapered off as she reached Brad's side.
The minister began the service, but Kara scarcely
heard his words as she kept her eyes trained on her
husband.

"... the ring is a symbol of eternity and constancy,
a visible symbol to all persons of the commitment you

have pledged to one another," the minister intoned, before instructing Brad to place the ring upon her finger.

Reaching into his pocket, Brad produced the unique rose quartz replica he'd had made for Kara. She smiled radiantly as he pushed it on her finger along with the softly brushed gold band.

Both waited breathlessly for the moment when the minister made the official pronouncement. The kiss overwhelmed their expectations. Now their marriage was real.

And so was the coming wedding night.

When they pulled apart, both could hear a distinctive sound rolling over the assemblage. Booms ricocheted through the area, indicating the mating of their ostriches. Glancing at Chuck bent over in laughter, Brad and Kara kept straight faces with immense effort.

Applause burst out from their guests as the minister withdrew his attention from the strange sounds that were growing steadily and tried to smile as though nothing were amiss. "I give you Mr. and Mrs. Bradley William Holbrook."

The reception passed rapidly. Well wishes were given along with numerous toasts. The cake was cut, then the guests wandered away. And soon they were alone.

Brad reached for Kara, pulling her close enough to feel her heartbeat, and recognize its accelerated pace. Fingering the simple, delicate lace of the dress bodice, Brad smiled, white teeth gleaming in the semi-darkness.

"Tillie's?"

Surprise mingled with the desire in her expression. "How did you know?"

"A little birdie told me?"

She chuckled, thinking of their "little birdies."

"There is one thing wrong with it, though," he continued.

"Oh?"

"It's still on."

He reached up to stroke her golden hair as the moonlight washed over her face. "I love you, Kara Holbrook."

Hot tears of joy threatened to spill past her shadowing lashes. "This time's forever, you know."

"And that contract's written across my heart," he promised, before slanting his head to take her mouth in an incredibly tender kiss.

Moonlight spilled across the disarray of her wedding gown as it lay puddled on the carpet. And somewhere Aunt Tillie smiled as the words of love carried through the room and into the sultry Southern night.

BRIDE'S BAY RESORT

UNLOCK THE DOOR TO GREAT ROMANCE AT BRIDE'S BAY RESORT

Join Harlequin's new across-the-lines series, set in an exclusive hotel on an island off the coast of South Carolina.

Seven of your favorite authors will bring you exciting stories about fascinating heroes and heroines discovering love at Bride's Bay Resort.

Look for these fabulous stories coming to a store near you beginning in January 1996.

Harlequin American Romance #613 in January
Matchmaking Baby by Cathy Gillen Thacker

Harlequin Presents #1794 in February
Indiscretions by Robyn Donald

Harlequin Intrigue #362 in March
Love and Lies by Dawn Stewardson

Harlequin Romance #3404 in April
Make Believe Engagement by Day Leclaire

Harlequin Temptation #588 in May
Stranger in the Night by Roseanne Williams

Harlequin Superromance #695 in June
Married to a Stranger by Connie Bennett

Harlequin Historicals #324 in July
Dulcie's Gift by Ruth Langan

Visit Bride's Bay Resort each month wherever Harlequin books are sold.

HARLEQUIN ®

BBAYG

MILLION DOLLAR SWEEPSTAKES

HARLEQUIN®

AMERICAN ◆ ROMANCE®

In Name Only

...because there are many reasons for saying "I do."

American Romance cordially invites you to a wedding of convenience. This is one reluctant bride and groom with their own unique reasons for marrying...IN NAME ONLY.

By popular demand American Romance continues this story of favorite marriage-of-convenience books. Don't miss

#624 THE NEWLYWED GAME
by Bonnie K. Winn
March 1996

Find out why some couples marry first...and learn to love later. Watch for IN NAME ONLY!

The Magic Wedding Dress

Imagine a wedding dress that costs a million dollars.
Imagine a wedding dress that allows the wearer to
find her one true love—not always the man she
thinks it is. And then imagine a wedding dress that
brings out all the best attributes in its bride, so that
every man who glimpses her is sure to fall in love.
Karen Toller Whittenburg imagined just such a dress
and allowed it to take on a life of its own in her new
American Romance trilogy, *The Magic Wedding Dress*.
Be sure to catch all three:

March
#621—THE MILLION-DOLLAR BRIDE

May
#630—THE FIFTY-CENT GROOM

August
#643—THE TWO-PENNY WEDDING

Come along and dream with Karen Toller Whittenburg!

*With only forty-eight hours to lasso their mates—
it's a stampede...to the altar!*

by Cathy Gillen Thacker

Looking down from above, Montana maven
Max McKendrick wants to make sure his heirs get
something money can't buy—true love! And if his two
nephews and niece want to inherit their piece of his
sprawling Silver Spur ranch then they'll have to wed the
spouse of *his* choice—within forty-eight hours!

Don't miss any of the Wild West Weddings titles!

www

Yo amo novelas con corazón!

Starting this March, Harlequin opens up to a whole new world of readers with two new romance lines in SPANISH!

Harlequin Deseo
* passionate, sensual and exciting stories

Harlequin Bianca
* romances that are fun, fresh and very contemporary

With four titles a month, each line will offer the same wonderfully romantic stories that you've come to love—now available in Spanish.

Look for them at selected retail outlets.

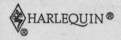 HARLEQUIN®

You're About to Become a Privileged Woman

Reap the rewards of fabulous free gifts and benefits with proofs-of-purchase from Harlequin and Silhouette books

Pages & Privileges™

It's our way of thanking you for buying our books at your favorite retail stores.

Harlequin and Silhouette— the most privileged readers in the world!

For more information about Harlequin and Silhouette's PAGES & PRIVILEGES program call the Pages & Privileges Benefits Desk: 1-503-794-2499

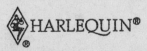

HARLEQUIN®

HAR-PP118